82

Ceil turned away impatiently and began to climb the stairs again.

'Don't you admire reckless women—just a little?' she asked him. They had reached the top of the tower and she turned to look at him.

'Reckless women are like fluttering moths—foolishly attracted to danger,' Jonathan told her.

'Really? And what about reckless men?'

'Reckless men, Ceil, are too smart to end up getting singed. They usually get what they want without landing in trouble.'

MOON OVER MOMBASA

BY

WYNNE MAY

MILLS & BOON LIMITED
ETON HOUSE   18-24 PARADISE ROAD
RICHMOND   SURREY   TW9 1SR

First published in Great Britain 1991 by Mills & Boon Limited

© Wynne May 1991

Australian copyright 1991

ISBN 0 263 12882 2

Set in Times Roman 10½ on 12 pt. 07-9108-48388 C

Made and printed in Great Britain

CHAPTER ONE

IT WAS a long, faded pink house with a white-pillared veranda running the full length of it. The dusty cement floor had long since lost the sheen of red veranda polish, and leaves and dried bougainvillaea flowers made scratching noises as they blew about in the light breeze. Strangely enough, the brightly coloured bracts which almost concealed the small flowers had kept their colour.

Ceil Downing went to lean against one of the white pillars and rested her ash-blonde head against it. She was wearing white cotton trousers, and their perfect fit made her legs look longer than ever. The word AFRICA and a picture of a beautiful southern red bishop, hovering next to a tawny nest, decorated the front of her black T-shirt.

Gazing at the garden, she thought how neglected it was, but that was not surprising. It was full of weeds, fluttering butterflies, dragonflies and birds, and she knew this was where she wanted to be—Kenya. Africa, where the sun sets like a huge red ball, she thought. Had her great-aunt worn a floppy straw hat, adorned with red cherries and black velvet ribbon, as she'd strolled about that garden?

Ceil's green eyes rested on what appeared to be a huge wild fig tree, to one side of the house, then went to the rubble of collapsed rocks which, in its day, must have been a rock garden. A number of succulents were

5

growing among the rocks, their flowers resembling orange-red spiders with long furry legs. The swimming-pool was covered with a dust-hardened plastic cover and it was packed with leaves and broken twigs. Like the house, the pool house was protected by scroll-like window guards.

Tom Mzima, the lawyer, was unlocking the wrought-iron gates in front of the french doors which, along with six others, led into various parts of the house. Ceil knew, without turning, that the white paint on all the woodwork was discoloured and panes of glass were filmed over with dust and grime.

In a soft drawling voice, Tom was saying, 'Everything is neglected, as you can see, but bear in mind that your late great-aunt was well past her prime and then in a nursing home for two years. Her health and that of her gardener had been failing for some time before that. The state in which the house now finds itself is the direct result of all this. Juma Kabaki had been her gardener and right-hand man for years and years and, later, became caretaker of the house. He has now gone to spend the rest of his days in his Kikuyu village in the Rift Valley. He too has inherited from the late Miss Downing and has already been advised. His son, Saba, works as a gardener in one of Nairobi's parks.'

Without turning, Ceil murmured, 'I realised why the house and garden are neglected.'

She was looking at the tower. She and Tom Mzima had already been to the top. Made of big slabs of beige stone, it reminded her of the tower of a small castle, even down to the battlements. It stood, alone, to one side of the house, and on their arrival, Tom had explained that it had been erected during the tense and troubled state of emergency in 1952 and that, in fact, many such towers had been built, particularly on farms and homesteads in lonely places. Fearing that her house might be set alight and burned to the ground—with her in it—her aunt had decided to have the stone structure built.

'As I explained when I showed you over the tower,' Tom was saying, 'it was built as a defence against possible marauding Mau Mau. Now, I am glad to say, it stands in peace, but, for all that, this is hardly the type of home suited to a young lady.'

He's challenging me, Ceil thought, and felt irritated. She turned to look at him with her beautiful, darkly lashed green eyes.

'The logical thing to do will be to join the tower to the house, by means of a wide gallery or something,' she decided. 'It will make a wonderful guest-house. I'll need an architect, of course. I intend to stay here, make no mistake.' She smiled. 'I was named after my aunt, as you've probably guessed. I've always hated the name Ceil. At school I got teased—you know...*seal*. Now, of course, the fact that I was named Ceil makes sense.'

'In what way does it make sense?' Tom Mzima's dark gaze seemed to be carefully evaluating her.

'Well, from her, I've not only inherited my name, but my own home in Africa.' As she spoke, she felt a rush of emotions. 'You know, Africa—along with the word India—has always attracted me like a magnet. When I come to think of it, it seems to have been on the cards that I come to Africa. And since my aunt has left money for this purpose, I'm longing to restore the property to all its original beauty. The thing which makes me feel so sad, though,' she added, 'is the fact that this is a house which has caused a great deal of friction in our family.'

'Why is this?' Tom sounded genuinely curious.

'Well, my parents—and for that matter half my relatives—were strongly opposed to my coming here. They were all for my selling my strange inheritance, without even having seen it.'

'Permit me to join forces and say that they were right. You would be better off selling the house and returning to England, where you belong.' He smiled. 'To leave the land of your birth takes courage—often foolish courage. I was educated in England and I yearned to return to my own country.'

'I didn't actually *want* to leave home—but I knew I had to,' Ceil explained.

Tom's face was a mask. 'I don't think you *had* to leave home. This house, in other words, could have been sold, along with everything in it, and, it is true what they say, without your even having seen it. You could have used the money and purchased another house in England, but,' he lifted his shoulders, 'you were curious, and since you seem bent on staying here, perhaps you should consider having someone to share the house with you? There are always people—reasonable, respectable people...'

'I don't think I'd like to share my house with anyone.' There was just a hint of exasperation in her voice now.

'Maybe you will change your mind. It will, after all, be a new experience for you, when you hear the hyenas at night.' A smile deepened the crease beside his mouth.

'*Will* I hear them?' She laughed.

'For sure you will.'

'Fortunately, I'm not subject to panic attacks. The hyenas won't worry me, I'm sure.'

'As usual, you have an answer for everything.' He spoke lightly, but Ceil had the feeling that he was serious. 'One of the first things I noticed about you was the fact that you are an effortlessly poised young lady and far more suited to London, I should imagine, than to a smallholding bordering a national game park.'

Listening to Tom Mzima, Ceil was thinking that he was wasting his breath, for she had no intention of being influenced by the reasoning of her great-aunt's lawyer, just as she'd had no intention of being influenced by the reasonable protests and, then, final angry outbursts of her parents before she had left England.

'I'll have to think of a name for the house,' she went on, 'since it doesn't appear to have one. Because of the tower, I think I'll call it Torre. You see, Mr Mzima, I have no intention of leaving Kenya.'

'Please—make it Tom.'

'Tom—and please, make it Ceil.'

He inclined his head. 'Ceil it will be. Now, let us come down to earth. You will be very much alone here—surely you can see that?'

'Privacy is always an attraction. If my great-aunt could live here—particularly when she was young—so can I. Besides, Tom, it's not so far from Nairobi. How far is it exactly?'

He thought for a moment. 'Let me put it this way. If you were to put this house on the market tomorrow, you could advertise something like this: Attractive Colonial-style house for sale. The house, which comprises...' he lifted his shoulders '...large lounge, dining-room, and so on, borders on the Nairobi national game park, which is situated within minutes of Nairobi, Kenya's bustling capital.'

'Well, there you have it! A few minutes from bustling Nairobi—within easy commuting distance——'

Interrupting her, he said, 'Although the game park is within sight of the town, your house, which leads off an out-of-the-way dirt road, has its back to Nairobi. It has absolutely no view of it whatsoever. You are as cut off here as you would be a thousand miles from anywhere. In other words, although it is only about eight kilometres from the city, under the circumstances it is far enough for it to be lonely and—let me stress—even dangerous. You must face this, if you are to live here alone.'

Taking the words 'under the circumstances' to mean that he was referring to the fact that the house was situated near to the game park, which covered about forty-four square miles and, except for elephant, was thick with game, including lions, she said, 'Because of wild animals? Is that what you're saying?'

'Because of two-legged animals, Ceil. I am referring to the odd loiterer, for instance—up to no good. You get these people.'

'But it can be dangerous anywhere. Oh, Tom, you're beginning to depress me—honestly!' Ceil spoke lightly and laughed a little, but she *was* beginning to feel depressed. 'Next you'll be telling me I should call the house Danger's Delight!'

'Danger is never a delight.' He gave her a steady look and she felt herself rebuked. 'You are, I think, inclined to be frivolous about serious matters. You have a lot to learn.' The hostility at the back of the remark was a shock.

Ceil glanced in the direction of the tower and all it had stood for. It was as formidable as a small castle, she thought. Had her great-aunt been frightened, as she had locked her house at sunset every evening and walked across to the tower, where she would bolt herself inside and then climb the spiralling wrought-iron stairs to the top? In that confined space, which was on three levels, there was a sitting-room, bedroom and tiny bathroom and a cupboard-sized kitchen.

'Well now...' Tom took a breath which Ceil could hear '...let me show you over your house. Once again, I think it is my duty to you—and to your family—to warn you to think, before you run away with yourself and move in here.'

Ceil realised that they had both been postponing that moment when she would step inside the house, and a shiver of expectation shot right through her.

They walked straight into the enormous lounge, from which there was a view of the spacious dining-room. She had expected the interior to be darkened by old-fashioned furniture, but here she was gazing at the most beautiful huge wicker sofas and armchairs. The upholstery and cushions were shabby, but she could imagine a future palette of colour and patterns. She would have the sofas and chairs re-covered in pink and tender green striped silk and then pile them high with over-stuffed cotton cushions. As she drifted about the room, Tom Mzima was a silent observer.

'Oh, so many books!' She crossed over to the alcoves on either side of the vast fireplace. As with just about everything else, the shelves would need fresh white paint. Her eyes went to the antique rug on the floor, which was in tones of light brick—almost pink, in fact—and blue. It was absolutely stunning, and it would blend in perfectly with bold chintz curtains in similar colours.

'It is an antique Heriz,' Tom said quietly. 'Your great-aunt was very fond of it.'

'It's beautiful!' Ceil held up a pair of brass candle-sticks. 'These will need a lot of work, but they're going to look wonderful on that low carved chest in front of the sofas on either side of the fireplace. I can just see it all. I'll get my mother to arrange a crate and send off my collection of Imari porcelain. It would seem that my aunt also had a passion for Imari.'

From across the room, she gave Tom a wide-eyed green look. 'This vase is just made for a mass of white lilies. You know something, Tom? It feels as if I've been set up and it will all be taken away from me. But as I stand here,' she went on, 'I can even imagine the aroma of breakfast cooking—bacon and eggs, coffee and burning toast.' She laughed lightly. 'I always end up burning toast. I can imagine myself taking my coffee out to the sun on the lawn, with the birds active all around me.'

After a moment she said, 'I hope I'm not boring you as I go on and on about everything?'

'Not at all. Take your time.'

'I was told my aunt loved to entertain, even when her health was failing.'

'Yes, that seems to be common knowledge in Nairobi. In her day, she entertained a lot. She became quite a legend.' Tom laughed softly. 'She enjoyed life. In her day, I was told, she used to like to motor to Coral Bay, a terrible road, I might add—three hundred miles of it. Later, of course, owing to the unrest, there would have been no entertaining and no drives to Coral Bay. People were tense.'

'I keep wondering why she never married,' Ceil said. 'I've seen photos of her—when she was young, that is. She used to send photos to England, and father has them all. She was fabulously beautiful. She always used to say, so my father said, that photography was a kind of journalism. Actually, she was right.'

'It was said that she was a natural platinum blonde.' Tom's dark eyes went to Ceil's silvery hair. 'Obviously you take after her, in more ways than one, I should imagine. About a man in her life—I believe there *was* a man. Nobody seems to know what happened to him.' He spread his hands. 'This was all long before my time, of course. I only came into her life after Mr Tyler, her lawyer, died. Funny thing—in some circles, people still talk about Miss Ceil Downing. Everybody knew about this—er—romance, and yet, to this day, what happened to him remains a mystery. Rumour has it that he wanted to marry her and move to another country, but she would have none of it. This house meant everything to her.'

Glancing around, Ceil said, 'Well, there seem to be masses of photo albums, letters and so on. I'm enormously curious to learn all about her. Maybe she left diaries and I'll find out, as I go through everything.'

The rest of the tour of the house revealed that most of the furniture was made from wood as golden as honey and had a wonderful patina. Ceil liked the barley-twist gateleg dining table, which was strangely related to white wicker chairs with blue and white cotton seats and fitted back-rest cushions. The base of the material was white, patterned with big blue elephants.

Later, Tom locked up and they went out to the car, which was parked at the foot of wide, shallow steps.

'I love it, Tom,' Ceil said softly, as he got in beside her. 'Don't try to talk me out of it.'

As they drove alongside the game park, Tom went on talking. 'This game park contains more species of birds than the entire British Isles, you know.' There was friendly mockery in his voice.

'You don't have to sell Africa to me, Tom. Like a moth drawn to a flame, I'm already hooked!'

He slackened speed and then stopped the car so that they could look across at two zebra stallions. It was obvious that they had been fighting and were about to do so again. Soon they were biting and kicking each other. Fine dust blew everywhere and there was the smell of it and dry grass.

Tom laughed. 'You want a fight—you get a fight! That appears to be what is going on over there.' He turned to look at Ceil. 'Well, you will be living right next door, practically, to lions and buffalo, to mention only two species of game. Apart from the harmless chorus of crickets and frogs at night, it will be nothing for you to hear the low grunt of a predator from your veranda. Fortunately for you, however, the park is fenced along two sides.' He drew the words out.

As was expected of her, she echoed, 'On two sides? Only two?'

'Uh-huh, that is right. At this very moment, Ceil, animals will be nudging each other and whispering—look, there goes our new neighbour—the one with the silver-white hair. Maybe, now and then, you will see rhino.'

'Oh, not on *my* side, I hope.' She kept her voice light, but she was beginning to wonder. 'Oh, look, Tom . . . aren't those vultures circling right over there?'

He turned his head. 'Yes, those are vultures. There must have been a kill. Some people say, when they see vultures circling like that, that the vultures are out window-shopping for food. You know, at night you will be well entertained, for you will most certainly hear these people.' He laughed at his own little joke.

'The sounds of the African night, in other words?'

'Yes, indeed. And so you can see for yourself that, while Nairobi is close to Kenya's wild-life, right here in this area, for you, it will be lonely.'

'Nevertheless, I can see Nairobi from here. Oh, I know my house is reached by a rough loop-road and that it has its back to Nairobi, but I really don't mind.'

Tom laughed, then said, 'To get back to your great-aunt. Apart from entertaining and motoring to Coral Bay, she used to grow vegetables and fruit, and, believe it or not, at one time she even ran a small poultry farm. Tell me, Ceil, do *you* intend to farm on a small scale?'

'No! That I can assure you. Everybody, though, dreams of a place like this, I should imagine. My aunt turned that dream into a reality for herself and, in turn, for me. I intend to live in the house and enjoy both it and the garden, but I intend to work in Nairobi. I can understand my aunt's passion for Kenya. In a way, I'm like one of those animals. I've now marked my territory and nothing, Tom, will change that.' Her thoughts were on the not so far distant flower-scented mornings when she would wake up in her own house.

'No? Maybe a man will come along, one fine day, to change all that, and then one day he will insist that you move on—with him.'

'That'll be the day!' She laughed.

'And so, like your legendary great-aunt Ceil Downing, after whom you were named, you intend to remain a spinster—for, man or no man in her life, she never married.'

'I didn't say that. I'm not moving, though, just because some man might come along and expect me to. I've got very strong views on that. Besides, I have a thirst for the sun. I'm here to stay.'

'Which is your way of telling me to shut up!' He laughed. 'Ah well, since I am losing ground and obviously no match for you, may I offer my help in dealing with those immigration documents? But bear in mind, don't take your house too seriously. It is only a house, after all. Don't end up being dictated to by a house. It could turn out to be a threatening relationship.'

They were now on the highway to Nairobi, and Ceil turned to gaze at the bougainvillaea which divided the carriageways. The ground was carpeted with the fallen bracts in shades of mauve, pink and purple. The footpaths on either side of the highway were provided with shade by jacaranda trees and cassias.

'While you are waiting for matters to be finalised you will, I take it, remain at the Norfolk Hotel?'

'Yes—that is, until I move into the house. There's a lot I'd like to do before I move. Sightsee, for one thing.'

Tom dropped her off at the half-timbered hotel where she knew by now, safaris had begun since its opening in 1904. It had used to be called the House of Lords. With its Tudor-style black beams and white stucco, the Norfolk made her think she was in Stratford-upon-Avon.

She waved to Tom as he pulled off. A plane banked over Nairobi, and she glanced up at it and was instantly a little homesick. Suddenly Tom stopped the car and reversed back to where she was standing.

'Worth mentioning, I believe. Early this century, lions were sometimes seen from the veranda of your hotel,' he told her.

She bent her head to talk to him. 'That must have been exciting. Now, instead, people and vehicles swarm in all directions, right? Instead of magnificent tawny lions growling and coughing there are all these cars doing it for them. Thanks for telling me. I'll be on the look-out, just in case!'

Well, she thought, as she entered her room, she had seen it. Her house! Her faded pink fortress which was in the vicinity of a game park and which was crying out for love and attention. A lot of attention, but then, in view of the fact that she had also been left a substantial amount of money—'to invest wisely and to use, as my niece, Ceil Downing, thinks fit'—this was not a problem and was high on the agenda.

The next two weeks were busy. Business matters concerning her strange and exciting inheritance were being finalised. In between going to Tom Mzima's office, Ceil was finding her way about the tree- and shrub-lined streets and boulevards of Nairobi. People turned to look at her fabulous ash-blonde hair, but as she was used to this wherever she went it did not bother her. She loved walking about and was fascinated by everything she saw, from the Kenyatta international conference centre to the pavement vendors selling fruit and flowers and little shops which sold medicines and concoctions in jars and displayed bunches of what appeared to be grasses, shrivelled roots, herbs and powders. Tom had warned her about handbag-snatching and stressed that she should not be careless, but she was excited and thrilled with everything.

She wrote an extra-long letter to her parents in which she described the house and Nairobi: 'Although there are no lions in the streets, there's still a lot going on here!'

Two mornings later, wearing jeans and a white silk top and looking tall, slim and stunning, she made her way to Tom's office. Tom was drinking coffee from a polystyrene cup.

'How are you, Ceil?'

'Wonderful! I even sing in my sleep.'

'So? Can I offer you coffee?'

'No, thank you. I had coffee a short while ago.'

'What can I do for you?' he asked, tossing the cup into a nearby basket.

'I'd like to get an architect to work out certain changes to the house, Tom.'

There was a short silence. Ceil noticed that, from his office, there was a view of the Jamia Mosque, which she had been visiting only a few minutes ago.

Tom lifted his dark eyes to look at her.

'Changes?'

'Yes—for one thing, I want to have the tower joined to the house.' She studied the expression on his face. 'I told you that, Tom.'

'Yes, you did, but surely, Ceil, the house is large enough as it stands?' He spoke with a certain impatience. 'Without incorporating the tower?'

She resented his tone. Who's paying for this? she asked herself. 'I may well want to use it. Maybe for guests from England. Who knows?'

He sighed so that she could hear it. 'Well, in that case, I can let you have the name of an architect. It has nothing to do with me, of course. Why not forget about an architect? In other words, I think you should endeavour to find a simple handyman to get on with the job. I feel sure even Jonathan would agree to that.'

'Jonathan?'

'The architect I have in mind. His offices are in Kamathi Street—Chaani, Caister and Balobo.'

'Jonathan is the...?'

'Jonathan is the Caister.'

'I see. Well, I'll arrange to come to your office when I'm ready, and, in turn, you can arrange to introduce me to this Jonathan Caister. Another thing, Tom, I know this is a bit much and you must be getting positively sick of me—but will you help me to buy a small car, now that everything is more or less settled?'

'Certainly—but be warned. Driving in Nairobi can be a nightmare. Why else did the city council put a fence down the middle of Haile Selassie Avenue?'

'Is *that* why?' she laughed. 'I wondered about that. I'll look forward to meeting the architect, Tom.'

'Although Jonathan is what can be safely described as a man who likes his own way, Ceil, already I am beginning to feel sorry for the guy.' Tom laughed to take the sting out of the words.

'Oh? In what way?' Ceil's voice was haughty.

'When it comes to that house, he will be in for a hard time, that's why.'

CHAPTER TWO

To WORK in Nairobi, from home, young woman
with computer experience. Phone Mombasa for
appointment. Interesting, unusual work. Computer, stationery and necessary office equipment
provided by company.

As she read the advert, Ceil immediately thought of
the tower and what a blessing it would be to work from
home where she would be in a position to supervise the
future alterations to her house.

She was still at the Norfolk Hotel, but would be
moving at the end of the month, which was only five
days away now. She was not just here for ninety days,
she had to keep reminding herself, when an alien's regis-
tration certificate would be all she needed. She was here
for good, and it was hard to believe that she was taking
this big step in her life.

When it had come to buying a good second-hand car,
Tom had helped her, but she would only take delivery
of the car after it had been resprayed. The vehicle had
had everything going for it, except for the colour, which
was a shabby beige. Because of the high accident rate,
mainly, she had opted for the colour red, which could
be easily seen.

At the time, Tom had laughed outright. 'Good
reasoning powers, my dear Ceil!'

Glancing at her watch, she reached for the phone and, after several frustrating moments of waiting, during which time she was told by Reception that the telephone system was often temperamental, especially when it came to rainy weather—and it *had* been pouring—she was put through to a firm called Computer Rewards and spoke to a man whose name was Abdel Khaled. After a time had been set for an appointment he said, 'Well, Miss Downing, I look forward to our forthcoming interview. By the way, the air service is quick and convenient and you will experience no problems.'

Ceil's green eyes were serious as she replaced the receiver. Had she done the right thing? Somehow she had always pictured Mombasa as a warren of narrow streets, dark alleys with wooden balconies hanging over them and intricately carved doors. Many of the women, she felt sure, would be shrouded and mysterious in garments such as the *rida* or *chador*, while the men would be clad in long white *kanzus* and have *kofias* on their heads. How would she fit into this scene, especially with her shoulder-length ash-blonde hair? Should she wear a scarf? A *skirt*? Suddenly she realised just how ignorant she was. She had known very little about Nairobi, let alone Mombasa. The very name Mombasa sent a thrill of expectation surging through her.

Lifting the receiver again, she made enquiries about flights to Mombasa and reserved a seat on a suitable plane. Nothing ventured, nothing gained, after all.

Things were beginning to move, she thought the next day as she hurried to board her plane. Tom had kindly picked her up and driven her to the airport with the arrangement that he would be there at sunset the following afternoon.

She had decided to wear white trousers with a white jacket, beneath which went a striped blouse in colours of rose, amethyst and emerald, and she exuded self-confidence and glamour—the image of a girl who knew what she wanted from life, in fact.

She controlled her impatience when she bumped into a man and then dropped the magazine she was carrying. As they both stooped to retrieve it, her bag slipped from her shoulder and, irritably, she adjusted the strap.

'Maybe in future you should look where you're going?' There was no anger, only amusement in the tone of his voice. 'It would, after all, be in your own interest. Did I hurt you?'

As she straightened, her gold earrings swung against her cheeks.

'No, you didn't,' she answered, thinking that he looked like some fictional hero, as their eyes met and held. *His* had the power to jolt. Dark eyebrows glistened above the bluest eyes she had ever seen. As she took the magazine from him, she said, 'Thank you. Maybe, on the other hand, *you* should look where you're going?'

He was, she noticed, wearing a lightweight business suit, and he had the body and looks which seemed to have been designed especially for it. He was carrying a briefcase and there was a nonchalant elegance about him, but when it came to business matters she could imagine his strong personality asserting itself in no uncertain manner. His unbelievably blue eyes were going over her.

'Tell me, are you for real?' he queried.

Tall, slim and haughty, Ceil said, 'Now, I wonder why you thought it necessary to say a stupid thing like that?' Don't try that magnetism on me, she thought, as she moved on.

A few minutes later he took the seat next to hers on the plane, and she could feel his vital presence before she turned to look at him. His smile was mocking and he had the assurance which stemmed from knowing he was attractive. There was just a trace of a dimple near the corner of his mouth.

'As you can see, *I do* make a point of looking in the right direction,' he told her.

Giving him a cool stare, she said, 'That must be very convenient for you, but I reserve the right to be touchy when someone sits next to me on a plane and quite obviously expects me to make frivolous conversation.'

'I should have known you'd say something like that.' He smiled again. 'But why fight the inevitable? By the way, as it happens, I'm just a respectable architect, on his way to see a difficult and excitable Italian client in Mombasa.'

'Really? You're not Jonathan Caister, by any chance?'

After a moment he laughed softly. 'But I don't believe this! How did you know?'

The plane was preparing for take-off and passengers were fastening their seat-belts. When they were airborne she heard him say, 'Look, I'm really curious. Tell me, how did you know who I was?'

She turned impatient green eyes on him. 'You've got it all worked out, haven't you? I make some utterly stupid joke about your being Jonathan Caister and you immediately climb in.' Looking at him, she was stunned by the realisation that she found him attractive *and* exciting.

'This isn't a joke, believe me. Are you going to tell me what all this is about?'

'Somebody mentioned the name of an architect to me, just the other day. For personal reasons, I remembered the name, but why I joked about it I just don't know. And now, why not face the inevitable? As it so happens, I'm the kind of person who likes to relax on a flight.'

Aloof and elegant, she reached for her magazine, which she had slipped into the pocket in front of her seat.

'Look, you can't do this to me.' He sounded frankly annoyed now. 'Who told you about me, anyway? I have a right to know, don't you think?'

To shake him off she said, 'My lawyer, Mr Mzima.'

'Tom?' He laughed outright. 'Well, well! What's all this about, anyway?'

Her eyes widened. 'Are you honestly Jonathan Caister?'

'I am honestly Jonathan Caister.' She watched him as he opened his jacket and slipped his hand into an inside pocket and then brought out his wallet and took out a card.

She did not take it from him, but looked at the names which appeared on it: 'Chaani, Caister and Balobo. Architectural Consultants.'

She shrugged. 'Small world.'

'I wonder why you found it necessary to disbelieve me?' As he put the card away he gave her a long, considering look. 'Anyway, since Tom isn't here to do the necessary, I'm Jonathan Caister.'

She smiled. 'And since Tom isn't here to introduce us formally, I'm Ceil Downing. I spoke to Tom about making possible architectural changes to my—er—house.' She was aware of a thrill. It sounded so strange to be referring to *her house*.

He continued to hold her gaze. 'In that case, why haven't you been in touch? Have you changed your mind about the alterations?'

'No, I haven't. I haven't moved into the house yet.' Without her intending it, her voice was low and seductive.

'I see. Well, when you're ready—you know my name and the number is in the book—or would you prefer a card?' She noticed the mockery in his eyes.

'A card would be—appropriate.'

A moment later she took it from him, aware that his fingers had brushed hers. When she had put it away she opened her magazine. Next to her, Jonathan Caister was reaching for his briefcase, then he opened it. Glancing sideways, she saw that he had begun to study what appeared to be a specification.

For the rest of the flight, which was rather bumpy, they had little to say to one another. Now and then, Ceil gazed out of the window, and felt excited as she saw the sun-gilded plains below. All this golden sunlight, she thought. No rain today.

As the plane prepared to land, Jonathan Caister snapped the catches of his briefcase. 'Are you going to Mombasa on business?' His voice was casual.

Ceil smiled up at the stewardess, who was checking to see if seat-belts had been fastened, before she said, 'I have an appointment with a Mombasa computer firm.

I'm being interviewed for a job, and if I get it, I'll be required to work from home, which will suit me very well. I don't know what the work's all about, of course. I was told they'd supply the computer, necessary office equipment, stationery, and so on. This is one of the reasons I want certain alterations done to the house. There's a tower, which I could use as an office. If I don't get the job—well, it's no big deal, really, because I'd intended to have this tower changed a little to act as a guest-house.'

'Why don't you just leave it as it is and work inside the house?' His blue eyes were no longer mocking, but serious.

'For the simple reason that there doesn't happen to be a study. There's a garden-room I could use, but...'

'Well, what's wrong with that? Or convert one of the bedrooms.'

'There are three bedrooms. I'll be using one of them and the other two will be used as guestrooms, for when I have guests from England.'

He laughed softly. 'You sound as if you're going to do a lot of entertaining. How were you thinking of joining this tower to the house—by means of a secret tunnel?'

'I don't know. A gallery or something. I mean,' she lifted her shoulders, 'you're an architect, you should know. That's why I want an architect—but maybe you're the wrong person for this.'

The plane was losing height. 'And maybe, on the other hand, I'm not. When are you going back to Nairobi?'

'I'm booked into the Castle Hotel for the night. I'm going back late tomorrow afternoon. I thought I might as well look around while I'm in Mombasa. I'm quite excited, actually.'

'Well, I'm booked in there for the next four nights. Perhaps we could meet for a drink and a chat this evening—before dinner?' His dark blue eyes met hers.

'I'd like that. I'm checking in to the hotel first, and then I'll be on my way to my interview.'

The plane was now racing along the runway and then coming to a standstill. Outside, the steps were moving into position and a moment later the door opened.

After going through formalities together, they went in search of a taxi, and then, as Ceil stood watching, Jonathan Caister and the driver appeared to be having an argument. As they settled themselves in the taxi, Jonathan explained, 'Always be careful with taxis. Some people are only posing as taxi-drivers, and others have meters that don't work, so when the time comes to pay you could find yourself in a heated argument.'

'I saw you arguing,' said Ceil. 'but that's not really surprising, I should imagine. Tom referred to you as a man who likes his own way.'

'Tom said that?' He turned to look at her. His low laugh was affectionate. 'Well, I guess you can say I'm a man who likes his own way when he knows he's right about something.'

As she looked out of the window, Ceil began to feel excited. The streets were bustling with activity,—full of people of all races: Africans, Arabs, wearing *kanzus* and *kofias*, Asians and Europeans. Whenever the taxi stopped the babble of languages could easily be heard.

'I didn't quite expect to see high-rise buildings,' she commented.

'In that case, you must see the old town. In fact, I'm going to plan my business appointments so that I can take you. We'll make time, before you leave. How's that?'

As she turned to look at Jonathan she was struck, again, by his strong good looks and the exciting texture of his tanned skin. 'I'd love that—if we can arrange something.'

By this time they had reached the Castle Hotel.

'I'm paying my share of the taxi,' Ceil said immediately.

Jonathan gave her an easy smile. 'This is my round. Forget it.'

'No, really. I'd find the situation very embarrassing, otherwise,' she insisted.

'Well, don't—and don't argue!'

She began to laugh. 'Let's not get into this. Now that you're going to act as my guide, I don't want to fight with you. I pay my share or no guided tour. OK?'

'You're not only reckless, you're stubborn.'

Before they were shown to their rooms, he said, 'Well, with hair the dramatic colour of moonstones, skin that looks like dusty-gold velvet, eyes that look like huge grapes and a mouth that was made for smiling, don't be *too* reckless. You might just find yourself in trouble. By the way, would you like to dine out tonight? There's a place on the North Mainland, where they serve excellent seafood.' Near his mouth that fascinating trace of a dimple appeared. 'Maybe you'd like to drink wine made from golden papaya fruit. How does that sound?'

Ceil smiled. 'How could I resist all this? It sounds nice, I must say.'

'Let's have a drink on the patio first, before we go,' he suggested. 'About six?'

'Meekly I submit to my fate,' she mocked. 'On the patio, then, about six.'

By the time Ceil arrived on the covered patio of the hotel at six that evening, Jonathan was already there. He looked relaxed and easy and his long legs were stretched out. When he spotted her, he stood up to greet her. He was incredibly handsome, she thought.

His dark blue eyes went over her face. 'Well, how did it go?'

'Oh, fine.' She smiled at him, as she sat down and crossed her legs. 'I got the job. I'm so excited!'

'And so we'll have to get busy on linking that tower to the house?' The way he said it sounded faintly mocking to her.

'Uhuh.' Let him mock, she thought. Suddenly she felt very successful—with the house and a job with a Mombasa-based firm and just *being* in Mombasa. Without really thinking, she said, 'I really feel like going out on the tiles.'

'On a debauch?' He spoke lightly, almost carelessly, as he beckoned to a bar-steward.

'Not a debauch.' Their eyes met. 'Just—to celebrate.'

'What would you like to drink?' he asked. 'A pink gin, to round off your success?'

'Frankly, I'd adore something cool and fresh.'

'I know just the thing.' As he gave their order Ceil sat studying him and thinking he looked like a dashing pilot instead of a serious architect.

He turned suddenly and caught her assessing green eyes. 'And so you've got the job?'

'Yes. The salary is good, but the thing which really appeals to me is that I'll be working from home.'

'What are the risks?'

His remark drew a curious glance from her. 'Risks?'

'What do you know about this—er—company?'

'Nothing, of course. It's called—it's all about computers. Besides, I enjoy taking risks—not that there are any risks involved here.'

'You hope? Just keep out of trouble.' Jonathan smiled suddenly. 'In fact, that's why I've taken you under my wing—to keep you out of trouble.'

'Oh, come!' she laughed.

'I have the feeling you have your head in the clouds.'

She decided to ignore his comment, and luckily the drinks arrived, then she went on, 'I'll be in a position to boss my workmen around by working at home. I think I'd have worked for less money, though, instead of working for better money in Nairobi. I feel it's terribly important to supervise the alterations I want done to the house.'

'Ah, that's better. Supervise—I don't like the word boss.'

'Well, supervise, then. Apart from having to supervise—or rather being in a *position* to supervise—I won't have to bother about travelling to Nairobi every day. You know, Jonathan,' she added, 'I thought I'd have to do a test or something, but this man at Computer—at this firm—seemed impressed enough to take me on right away.'

'What's his name?' Jonathan asked. 'And did he explain what the work was all about?'

'Well, of course.' Ceil reached for her glass.

He laughed softly, but there was a hard edge to the sound. 'Let me guess. You don't really know what you're landing yourself in, do you?'

She decided to beat about the bush. After all, it had nothing to do with him. 'I'll be doing research. In other words, I have to gather data for certain people.'

He sat back and regarded her. 'Listening to you, Ceil, I'm already beginning to worry about you. Do you always leap into everything?'

'It sounds as if I'm being put through the third degree!' She laughed, but she was beginning to feel more than just a little niggled.

'You don't seem sure about this work. What kind of data?' He sat back and watched her with cool, barely concealed amazement.

Ceil's irritation threatened to grow into anger. At this stage, anyway, she did not want to tell him that she would be managing—on her own—a section under the title of Computa-mate. She would, in other words, be handling the introductory advertising campaign for this service in Nairobi and, in turn, forwarding the necessary questionnaires—at a fee, of course—to people who had been interested enough to write in. She would be, in fact, gathering data for the future meeting of couples. It was nothing like she had expected, but the salary was good and she would have no travelling expenses to meet, into the bargain. What was even more inviting was the idea that her hours of working would be flexible.

'What does it matter to you what kind of data?'
Although she laughed lightly, her grape-green eyes were
beginning to slant. 'Let's just say I have to load the computer with certain information and thereby—er—predict
which—mm—people should meet which people. It's all
on a statistical basis. One can then calculate which...'
She broke off. 'But why are we talking about this?'

'Obviously you don't *want* to talk about it.'

'No, I don't. I just want to sit here and enjoy my good
luck and watch the busy life of Mombasa go by from
the patio. Besides, you can't really want to know.'

'I do want to know. I wouldn't be asking otherwise,
would I? I'm trying to work out what a Mombasa-based
company wants with the services of a person based in
Nairobi—and working from home.'

'This is ridiculous!' She shook her head and laughed
a little. 'Maybe because it's so simple that it defies a
simple definition.'

'Well, I hope you know what you're letting yourself
in for. The important thing for you to realise is that if
it's something shady you won't find sympathy from the
police, and you're a long way from home, Miss
Downing.' There was an edge to Jonathan's voice, which
she resented.

'I'm really not in the mood for all this,' she told him.

'Whether you're in the mood or not, let me put you
into the picture, the way I see it. You refer, vaguely, to
certain information. What is this information? The important thing for you to realise is that there are a lot of
sharks in the world. Don't rush into the first job you're
offered. It could be dangerous for you—but, just by

listening to you, I gather that you seem to thrive on danger.' His blue eyes took her apart.

'Well, a little danger is always stimulating, don't you think? Tom suggested I call the house Danger's Delight,' she added.

'Obviously he has you sized up.'

Although *he* was smiling Ceil could barely suppress the anger which was now surging through her. 'Do you know something, Jonathan? You're beginning to put me off having dinner with you.'

'And that would never do. In any case, you have two choices. Stay here and have a boring dinner on your own at the hotel or do something really exciting—by crossing the Nyali Bridge and going to enjoy some wonderful seafood on the North Mainland.'

'How do we get there?' she asked. 'I mean—what form of transport?'

'I always hire a car when I'm in Mombasa.'

'You sound as if you come to Mombasa quite often?' she queried, her anger fading.

'I come on business.'

'Have you ever spent a holiday here? I should imagine there's a lot to see and do.'

'No, I haven't. I once spent a few days at Diani Beach, among the coconut palms and the other flamboyant trees. There's a reef and a magnificent beach. It's a great place for a honeymoon, actually.'

The remark came as a jolt—like his intensely blue eyes—as she realised, suddenly, that he might be married.

'I take it you're speaking from personal experience? Is that where you spent your honeymoon?' Her voice was very casual.

He smiled and lifted one shoulder. 'No, but the idea has become seductive. It's on the south coast and quite unspoiled and uncrowded. An ideal spot.'

'And you're thinking of planning a honeymoon there?'

He laughed. 'So far I've managed to escape thinking about a honeymoon, but the day will come, no doubt. What about you?' His eyes went to her left hand. 'Am I to take it that there's just you and this house with a tower?'

'Because you don't see two rings?' She held out her hand, and her voice was mocking. 'That doesn't mean much these days, does it?'

'You're right, of course, it doesn't.' He made a dismissive gesture, then pulled back his sleeve to look at his watch. He lifted his eyes again. 'Whose house is it? Yours? Or his?'

'It's my house.'

He went on looking at her and then he said, 'Are you really going to call the house Danger's Delight?'

'No, of course not.' She laughed.

'Why don't you call it Mnarani—which means the place of the minaret or tower?'

'Mnarani—I like that, Jonathan. Thank you, you've just christened my house.' She lifted her glass.

'Good. By the way, would you like me to add a minaret?' His voice was teasing.

'Just you think of a way of joining the tower to the house. A tunnel is out!'

'And so I'm hired?' His blue eyes were full of mockery.

'That depends on how much you're going to charge,' Ceil answered carelessly.

'Let's put it this way—I'm not cheap.' He glanced at his watch again. 'Is there anything you'd like to do before we leave? I think it's time to make a move.'

After she had collected a light silk jacket, they went out to the car which he had hired. The air, Ceil noticed, was warm and clinging.

Jonathan opened the door for her and then went round to his side and got in. He turned to look at her. 'Well, how does it feel—being in a sauna, fully clothed? Is it hot enough for you?'

'I can't get over it!' She laughed.

'Let me fill you in.' He started the car. 'We're going to cross over to North Mainland by means of the Nyali Bridge. At one time, crossing was by small rowing boats, so we're lucky—although perhaps, for the sheer danger of it, you would have preferred to row across?'

She decided to ignore that and when she spoke her voice was cold and polite. 'I had no idea Mombasa was so steamy—although I might have known.'

'It's steamy in more ways than one,' he told her, 'since it's essentially a sailors' town. That's why a reckless girl like you needs looking after.'

CHAPTER THREE

THE NIGHT-SPOT came as a pleasant surprise to Ceil. It was called the Camel and, from the open terrace, they looked across the shivering waters of Mombasa harbour towards the old town, which nestled above the old dhow harbour, its entrance dominated by the brooding bulk of Fort Jesus. A small band was playing soft, romantic music and one or two couples were dancing.

Turning to Jonathan, she said, 'How clever of you to arrange for the moon to be hanging over the water.'

He gave her a mocking smile. 'It took a bit of negotiating, but it does look good, doesn't it?'

At the end of the main course, Jonathan ordered desserts and then, as they waited for them, he asked Ceil whether she would care to dance.

To begin with, he held her lightly, but was soon holding her closer to him—and then closer, so that she could feel his breath against her cheek, and his body as it moved to the music. In her narrow black skirt, which she was wearing with a frothy white blouse, she felt glamorous and aware of herself—and of him. Her olive and saffron silk jacket was draped over the back of her chair and it did not look as though she was going to need it.

Suddenly he held her away from him and looked into her eyes. 'And so, Ceil Downing, you're very much tied up in Nairobi?'

'You mean, of course, with a man?'

'If you want the truth, yes.' There was a wealth of meaning in the tone of his voice.

'And the fact that I'm not wearing his ring!' She laughed. 'I'm not in a hurry.'

'For someone who's only been in Kenya for a short time, you've certainly got around—unless you brought him with you?'

'No, I didn't bring him with me.' His male arrogance had aggravated her, so she strung him along. If he wanted to believe these things of her, that was fine by her.

'I was just thinking,' she went on, 'this is really good for business, don't you think? This getting to know each other before you start on my plans.'

'You reckon?' Jonathan laughed softly. 'That's a teasing question, after all.'

'Well, don't you?'

After a moment he said, 'The point is—how well do you want to get to know me?' His blue eyes were suddenly coldly speculative.

Ceil found the strong sexual overtones disturbing and realised, with a sense of shock, that she hardly knew him. It didn't mean to say that, because he had the trace of a dimple near the corner of his mouth and was devastatingly handsome, he was all right.

At that point the music stopped and they went back to their table, where she studied him when she thought he wasn't looking. Once, when their eyes happened to meet, she found herself thinking that, while he obviously found her attractive, he was suspicious of her. Well, that cut two ways. She was suspicious of him too now.

He gave her a long direct look that appeared to be summing her up and then dismissing her in one brief second. 'I don't think it's a good idea for me to do your plans,' he said.

'Well, fine. I'll speak to Mr Chaani or Mr Balobo. It's no big deal.' She was beginning to feel angry, but she tried not to show it. Spitefully, she added, 'I might even draw them myself.'

He laughed at that. 'Just like you do everything else? In a hurry and without much thought?'

Ceil sat back and gazed at him. 'You appear to be in an unpleasant frame of mind. Would you mind telling me why?'

'I'm saying perhaps you should get someone else to work out something to suit you. I'm not sure I have the time—or the inclination, for that matter. I'm being honest with you.'

She was stunned at his rudeness. 'I think you're being highly unprofessional *and* abrupt. I find this very dismaying, especially as you've been stringing me along that you *were* interested. Actually, it was on these grounds that I decided to accept your invitation to dine here.'

'Really?' His smile was mocking. 'Anyway, I wasn't stringing you along. That's not a habit of mine.'

Her green eyes were hot with helpless anger. She glanced down at the dessert which had been placed in front of her. 'What is this dessert you've ordered?' She lifted her lashes.

'It's *kulfi*—I told you that. It's rich, saffron-flavoured ice-cream. You'll like it. Afterwards, I suggest black coffee, spiced with ginger.'

'That's a good idea. Perhaps that's exactly what you need—a cup of strong black coffee, spiced with ginger.'

'To counteract that papaya wine?'

She shrugged. Huffily she watched him as he ordered it and then she could hold back no longer. 'Is it something I've said—or done—to put you in this ugly mood?'

He thought for a moment. 'Has it ever struck you how vulnerable you are?'

'I'm not sure I understand you, but in any case, Mr Caister, I'm not just off the ark, you know. I don't think I'm—vulnerable.'

'That's OK, then.' He sat back in his chair and looked at her though narrowed eyes. 'Tell me, what do you think of this place?'

Ceil shrugged. 'It's not exactly a place for disco fans, is it?'

'Are you a disco fan?' he asked.

'I don't mind disco—and you?' Her voice was still cool.

'I'm getting too old to go to discos,' he mocked. 'So you expected a disco?'

'I did, as a matter of fact.' This was true, and this was why the Camel had come as a pleasant surprise.

'But I don't need that aggravation in my life, I'm afraid.' He sounded almost hostile.

'What do you mean—aggravation? I'm not sure I understand.' Ceil's voice was quiet and controlled.

'I mean, Miss Downing,' he drew her name out sarcastically, 'I don't particularly relish the idea of going somewhere where I have to be on the alert in case someone decides to hassle the girl I happen to be with— in this instance a glamorous blonde with hair the colour of moonstone who's not just off the ark! There's always that possibility, and the possibility that things could get out of hand.'

'Jonathan,' she sighed. 'I have enjoyed myself tonight—up until a short while ago, that is.'

'But you'd have preferred something a little more on the dangerous side, is that it? Something which you could put down to experience—you know, one of those dives in a narrow, winding street, where we could have eaten Arab food and danced to hot disco music? Some place open until four in the morning and where, to protect you, at some stage I could have ended up having to fight?'

Ceil was really furious now. 'Aren't I worth fighting over?' she baited. Why were they going on like this? she wondered a little frantically. Had they both had too much wine? But no. She had wanted to try the wine, but, since she had found Jonathan to be just a little too exciting for her own good, she had not drunk much. Somehow she got the idea that he had, at some point in the evening, decided he didn't like her. Possibly because he believed she was living with a man. Well, that was fine by her. Let him think what he liked. How dared he sit there and jump to conclusions about her?

In a dangerously soft voice he was saying, 'Are you daring me, Ceil?'

'Daring you? Oh, for goodness' sake! Surely I don't have to dare *you* to do anything?'

Ceil could see that he was feeling particularly aggressive now.

'Of course,' he said, 'we could always go on some-where. The Mombasa Mamba Pit is as good a place as any.'

'I didn't come here to put up with your hostility, Jonathan.' She reached for her silk jacket. 'Just take me back to the hotel this minute. I've had enough.'

By the time she got into the car she felt she had herself under control, but she was, in fact, still trembling with anger.

As they drove through the heavy sleepy darkness she eventually had the feeling that they were not heading in the right direction. Turning to look at him, she said, as calmly as she could, 'Jonathan, take me back to the hotel. I don't know what you have in mind, but, whatever it is, forget it.'

'These alleyways were made just wide enough to take a loaded camel. Just hold thumbs.' He turned to look at her.

Her voice rose. 'Even I can see this is what they call the waterfront! I'm tired, Jonathan, and it's very late.'

'You'd better start reviving, in that case. The Pit is open till four.'

At first she thought he was merely trying to frighten her, and then he pulled up next to a shabby building with a sagging balcony. Yellow light-bulbs blinked on and off.

A cold rage started in her. 'Take me back!' she snapped.

'What if I refuse?' He was smiling now. His eyes lingered with lazy insolence on her mouth.

When he kissed her, his mouth was surprisingly gentle, and she remained calm and still, but her heart was thudding. Don't struggle, she thought. After all, you don't know this staggeringly handsome animal with his unbelievable blue eyes—and neither does Tom, it would appear. Apart from anything else, though, she didn't like the area in which she found herself.

He released her. 'What's the problem? Don't you want to dance to some *mean* music?'

'I'm not going in there. What do you take me for?'

'In that case, Ceil, sit here, until I get back!'

For a moment she thought she was going to have hysterics. 'How dare you do this to me?' She spoke in the carefully modulated voice she always used when she felt out of her depth.

'All the sailors patronise the Mombasa Mamba Pit,' Jonathan went on. 'You know, all the boys just off S.S. *Danger's Delight*. I bet Tom didn't suggest you named your house that for nothing.'

'Leave Tom out of this, take me back to the hotel. When I want to visit a dive like this, I'll let you know.'

'What's made you change your mind? Obviously you wanted me to get into a brawl, so come along.'

Ceil tried not to scream at him, but ended up shouting. 'I'm not going! I have no desire to see you brawling!'

'In that case, I'll go alone. You might well have the pleasure of seeing me thrown out head first. How does that appeal?'

'Go, then, but if you leave me here, I'll take your car!'

'How?' he laughed. 'Tell me, how, since I'll have the key?' She watched him as he took the key from the ignition and slipped it into his pocket.

Suddenly, she felt she'd had more than she could take, and she opened the door and stepped out. Stooping to look at him through the open window, she said, 'I don't have to put up with any of this. I'll find my own way back.'

Jonathan was out of the car in an instant, and came after her. Grabbing her by the shoulders, he swung her round to face him. 'You're a long way from home, Ceil, and I don't just mean that house of yours on the outskirts of Nairobi. I'm trying to make out what makes you tick.'

'Really? Would you mind telling me what all this is about—what makes me tick?' She pushed him away. 'And take your hands off me!'

'Look, you arrive in Kenya, you find yourself a house and a boyfriend to share it. You allow a perfect stranger to take you across the dark waters of the Mombasa harbour, where you get to work by goading him to take you to some wild disco and even getting into a fight.' The savagery in his voice shocked her.

'I didn't goad you!' she retorted furiously.

'You said, "Aren't I worth fighting over?". That's what *I* call baiting a guy.'

She slapped his face then.

'Get back into the car!' he demanded.

'No! I don't want to be with you. How does nice Tom Mzima know a pig like you?' Her voice was scathing and choked.

'Why don't you ask him? Come on, Ceil. I'll take you back to the hotel.' His voice had changed.

'Now that you've had your fun, is that it?'

She walked back to the car and got in. Her heart was hammering and she took a long, calming breath.

On the drive back Jonathan said softly, 'I guess I should say I'm sorry. Well, I *am* sorry.'

'Oh, go to hell!' she snapped.

To crown everything, thunder was rumbling in the distance, and it was a relief to see the Castle Hotel again.

Ceil thought she wouldn't sleep but, feeling exhausted and used-up, she did.

In the morning, there was a knock on her door and, believing it was a maid, Ceil opened it and found herself looking into Jonathan's amazing Indian Ocean blue eyes.

'What do you want?' she asked aggressively.

'To make peace and to apologise again and to remind you that before I blew everything last night we'd made a date to visit the old town.'

Her eyes glittered at his insolence. 'There've been a few changes since last night. I have no desire to see you again. You have the nerve to turn up here as if nothing has happened! Do you think I'd go to the old town with you, after the way you behaved last night? You must be joking. You're so arrogant, it's unbelievable!'

'What happened, Ceil, is that I guess you just rubbed me up the wrong way.'

'I rubbed you up the wrong way?' She laughed sarcastically. 'But to pacify me, you apologise! I can't get over this!'

'Maybe I went to extremes, but it defeats me why we can't forget the whole stupid episode—because it *was* stupid, let's face it. Things just got out of hand.'

His remark earned him another furious look. 'Things got out of hand? You were going to take me to a dive along the waterfront!'

'Well, I didn't, so why don't we just forget the whole thing?'

'I'll tell you why—because I've completely lost trust in you,' she told him. 'And now, if you don't mind, I have things to do.'

'Ceil, wait! Maybe I was wrong, but I was under the impression——'

'Maybe you were wrong?' she cut in. 'I like that! You jolly well were wrong!'

'So I was wrong—but let's face it, you don't just go off with some guy you've just met to a night-spot in Mombasa, and you most certainly don't go around passing remarks like, "Aren't I worth fighting over?"'

Ceil was stunned by his words and the impression she had apparently made on him.

'I accepted you at face value, Jonathan,' she snapped, 'not to mention the fact that Tom spoke well about you. And now, after all this, you have the audacity to ask me to go to the old town with you!'

Suddenly he smiled. 'I've been to a lot of trouble to change my appointments so that we could be together until your plane leaves this afternoon. Come on, say yes!'

'And hate myself afterwards?'

'I was going to do all the right things,' he went on. 'I was going to show you the Mandhry Mosque, which is probably the oldest mosque in Mombasa. We were going to walk about and look at the shops, markets and gold- and silversmiths at work. I'd planned to buy you a silver anklet.' His eyes were mocking. 'Maybe even a carpet from Iran—who knows? Certainly I'd have insisted that we bought coffee from an Arab coffee vendor, which he would pour from a brass coffee-pot.'

'So you think a visit to the old town looks bright?'

'Yes.' His eyes held hers.

'Well, you have another think coming, Mr Caister!'

'I'll be on the patio at ten,' he told her. 'I'm hoping you'll be there.'

'Let me give you some advice,' she retorted. 'Don't count on it!'

CHAPTER FOUR

GOING from one exciting shop to another, Ceil spent the morning shopping and enjoying the vibrant street life. In the end she had to buy a sisal shopping basket to hold all her parcels: a vast Arab caftan, a length of brightly coloured cotton, a gemstone bracelet from the Treasure Cove and elaborately coloured bead earrings.

As it happened, Jonathan was at the Reception desk when she got back to the hotel, and he turned to look at her as she asked for her key. Glancing at the shopping basket, he said, 'You've been busy, by the looks of it.'

On the spur of the moment, she decided not to allow the events of the night before to overshadow her pleasure at being in Mombasa.

'Yes, I have.' She held out her wrist. 'How do you like my bracelet? I couldn't resist it and decided to wear it.'

As he bent his head to look at the bracelet, she studied his face, and, although she could still feel the anger of the night before, she liked what she saw and decided to forgive him.

'Very nice,' he said, as he straightened. 'Well, have you made up your mind about the old town, or shall I make it up for you?' She saw the mockery in his eyes.

After a moment she said, 'I'll have to drop off these parcels first. I don't know why, after last night, but I'll come.'

Directly she reached her room, she applied cleansing cream to her face and then moisturiser and fresh make-up. Her hair was loose and she combed it back and secured it with a clasp. On an impulse, she removed her gold earrings and fitted the beaded ones she had just purchased.

Wearing jeans now, and a dark blue loose-knit shirt, Jonathan was waiting at reception.

'I hope you're wearing comfortable shoes?'

'I am, actually.' Ceil held out a sandal-clad foot.

His eyes went to her earrings. 'Another good buy?'

She laughed a little. 'I couldn't be more thrilled than if they were Venetian glass from Murano. I love the colours. Aquamarine, sea-green and olive; just the same as this top I'm wearing, actually. By the way, will I be all right in trousers?' she added. 'I wouldn't like to anger or embarrass the Muslim community.'

'You're fine,' he told her. 'Touristy, but nicely covered, which is the main thing.'

As they walked in the direction of the exit he said, 'It's only fair to tell you, I haven't the faintest idea what lay behind those yellow lights last night. I just drove until I saw a suitable façade.'

'What?' Ceil widened her eyes. 'Are you telling me there *wasn't* a Mombasa Mamba Pit?' She began to feel humiliated. 'Oh, Jonathan, you devil! How could you have done that to me?' Suddenly she found herself laughing. 'I shouldn't laugh,' she said, after a moment. 'It's not funny.'

'Ceil, let's consider the incident ridiculous. Last night was another story.'

They went outside and into the heat and the alleyways of the old town.

Some of the shops, Ceil found herself thinking, had been around a long, long time.

'There's one thing I would love to own,' she said, 'and that's a brass-studded Arab chest. I wonder how I could arrange it, Jonathan? Would they forward it to Nairobi, do you think?' She turned to look at him.

'I can always get you a brass-studded chest in Nairobi,' he told her. 'If we'd had more time, I could have arranged for you to visit a small factory which makes them for export to the Gulf. Maybe next time.'

The pavements were crammed with material, and they squeezed past bolts of purple, cerise, pink, yellow and rust-coloured fabric, all roped together and secured to cement pillars.

Jonathan did not take his hand from her arm. 'Let's go inside and buy you a *kanga*. You deserve one.'

'First you want to buy me a silver anklet and now it's a *kanga*! Do I deserve one because I forgave you?'

They went into the shop, where two overhead fans revolved lethargically in the gloom, hardly moving the warm, heavy air. Ceil saw the *kanga* she wanted almost immediately.

'That was quick work.' There was mockery in Jonathan's voice. 'I had visions of being here for at least an hour.'

'I fell in love with the colour,' she told him.

The assistant left them for a moment and when he came back he said, 'What about a *kikoi* for your husband?' He held up a piece of purple cloth.

Laughing, Ceil said, 'How is it worn?' Her eyes went to Jonathan.

'Like this—see?' The assistant wrapped the material around his waist.

Her amused eyes went back to Jonathan. 'What do you think of the colour, Jonathan?'

'I like it. Thank you, darling.' He gave her his sexiest look. 'I'll wear it at the poolside.'

When they were back on the pavement, she said, 'You would have thought he would have noticed that I'm not wearing a ring. After all, you did.'

'Perhaps because I was far more interested than he was.'

Ignoring his remark, Ceil went on, 'I do have a pool, you know. At the moment it's covered by a dirty old pool-cover. I haven't seen what's underneath yet, and I'm dreading it. At any rate, I intend to restore it, and so you can wear your *kikoi*, as you recline on a fancy floral chaise.'

'The tradition is to wear a *kikoi* with long cotton trousers. Do I have to be traditional, or do I show my legs?' he teased.

'Please yourself. If you have good legs—well, show them. To get back to the pool, though. When I first saw it, I began to ask myself whether I should have it filled in, and done with it, but since I was left money to pay for renovations and repairs to the house I've decided otherwise.'

There was a short silence and then Jonathan said, 'It sounds as if I'm walking around the old town with an heiress.'

She decided to tell him. After all, he would get to know sooner or later. 'You might as well know, I suppose—I inherited this house and a somewhat unusual and lovely collection of furniture from the great-aunt after whom I was named—Ceil Downing. I'd only met her a few times, when she visited England. Then one unforgettable day I found myself the owner of a house in Kenya.'

He was visibly surprised. 'So that's the set-up? I've been wondering.'

Ceil looked at her watch. 'I've enjoyed all this very much, Jonathan. I'm becoming worried about the time, though. I have a plane to catch, remember.'

'How could I forget, since it will be taking you away from Mombasa? Anyway, the chances are we'll do something like this again.'

'I'd love that. Maybe we could visit Fort Jesus—I'm absolutely fascinated. We could walk round the ramparts and look——'

'At the views of the harbour and the moon on the water?' he cut in. 'In the meantime, though, there'll just be time for a quick lunch.'

'Are you sure there's time?' she queried. 'I don't want to have to charter a plane.' She laughed lightly.

'We'll make time,' Jonathan told her.

He took her to a place where high-backed, hand-carved wooden chairs formed part of the Asiatic décor. They had traditional Indian food, and then Jonathan drove Ceil to the airport, after they had been back to the hotel for her belongings.

She felt a moment of bleak depression at the thought of saying goodbye and then going home to her lovely but very lonely house.

'I'll look out for that Arab anklet,' he told her, 'and I'll bring it back for you.' His blue eyes remained on her face as he spoke.

'You'd like that, wouldn't you? Seeing me with eyes downcast and wearing a silver anklet.'

'Enjoy your flight, Ceil. I hope it's not too bumpy.'

'Bumps don't bother me,' she assured him.

'We'll see what we can do about joining that tower to the house without having to resort to a tunnel,' he teased.

'Oh, before I go, I'm going to call the house Mnarani, Jonathan. We'll drink a toast to that when you get back.'

'Great.' He smiled lazily. 'I'll be seeing you.'

At the top of the steps to the plane Ceil turned and waved, and a few seconds later she fastened her seat-belt. Somebody had left a newspaper in the pocket in front of her seat and, without really thinking, she reached for it.

As the plane prepared for take-off, her eyes scanned the front page, then her heart skipped a beat when she saw a picture of Jonathan. She began to read.

> Jonathan Caister and his colleagues at Chaani, Caister and Balobo are helping to solve housing problems in this country. There is a need for new practical designs and the revamping of certain run-down areas.

Putting the paper back into the pocket, she allowed herself to speculate. Going over the whole episode, she realised that she had been attracted to Jonathan Caister from the moment they had collided at the airport in Nairobi.

She began to feel excited. She had done the right thing in forgiving him for frightening her on the waterfront.

By the time the plane touched down the heat had left the sun, and Tom was there to meet her.

CHAPTER FIVE

ARRIVING back in Nairobi meant days of hectic activity for Ceil. Since she had now taken delivery of her car, she had been driving out to the house nearly every day. She vacuumed, polished, washed down walls and dusted.

Abdel Khaled phoned to explain that he had arranged for a desk, office equipment, stationery and a magic box of circuits and silicon chips to be sent to her. Laughing at his own little joke, he'd added, 'In other words, your computer, which, as you know, would be useless without the necessary software. Everything, therefore, will be delivered to your home, on a day which will suit you, and I now await instructions as to how my source of supply will find this house. This is all that is holding us up.'

Ceil explained that she would be at the house on Monday and Tuesday all day, and would be on the lookout for the vehicle.

The computer, desk, filing cabinet and stationery had gone straight into one of the bedrooms. Although there were already two desks in the house, she had thought it best not to argue when Abdel Khaled had phoned to advise her that another would be arriving, with the other items.

On the day she had moved into Mnarani there had been a certain restlessness in the air, and this was followed by a violent rainstorm. Sheets of rain obscured the garden and hammered down on the roof, and it was a strange experience—and even frightening—listening to the noise on the corrugated-iron roof. Directly the storm passed over, the sun reappeared and glittering raindrops clung to the leaves. The neglected garden was suddenly attractive. Several shrubs were flowering. A large wild tree was in full bloom and the pink flowers, which had dropped earlier, or been battered there by the torrential downpour, created a colourful carpet on the grass. A well-trimmed and manicured lawn would have to take over from the grass at a later stage.

Soon everything was shimmering with heat. Standing on the pillared veranda, Ceil thought, I'm going to be alone in this house tonight, and all the other nights to come.

Her mind drifted to her childhood and her mother's constant warnings. Ceil, your curiosity could get you into a lot of trouble one day.

Turning away from the view of the garden, Ceil went inside. Looking at the room, which was going to need so much attention and fresh colour introduced into it, her eyes rested on the purple irises and pink and gold roses which she had bought in Nairobi and arranged in a large cut-glass vase. By the time she was finished with it, this room—along with all the other rooms in the house—was going to be exciting and beautiful.

Lock up carefully at night, Tom Mzima had warned, and, Ceil, you can't be too careful these days. You can't play around. Life will never be what it used to be, here or anywhere else in the world. You should know that, just by having watched television alone, not to mention what the media have to report in the newspapers.

After that first week, during which there had been that violent rainstorm, the anxiety attack which she had experienced was a thing of the past. Although she often felt the kind of tension which stemmed from being alone, she began to feel good. She had done the right thing by coming to Kenya.

Abdel Khaled had sent her a parcel of questionnaires. These, he explained in a separate letter, had been completed by clients and therefore were ready for the information to be loaded into her computer. This was to get her going until results were forthcoming from the advertisements which, he felt sure, she had now probably placed in a local magazine and newspapers.

> I expect you to be pulling in your own clients in the very near future, but these questionnaires, which are all in English, will get you going in the meantime. Do not hesitate to be in touch, should you experience any problems.

In any case, as previously arranged, questionnaires not answered in English would be forwarded to Mombasa, Ceil thought.

Sitting on the veranda one morning, she studied the questionnaires and gave a resigned shrug. She'd certainly landed herself a strange position, she mused, but working from home had its uses.

> Membership lasts for one year. For results of your first computer run call us within seven to ten days of joining. Subsequent computer runs during the year will be free of charge. Should you meet your mate and no longer need our services, kindly let

us know immediately. Your details will then be removed from the computer. Complete the questionnaire and include your membership fee.

The rest covered such details as surname, Christian names, address, phone numbers—home and business—age, sex, religion, occupation and marital status. Other questions related to height, weight, physical disability—if any—physical type, appearance, leisure and holiday preferences.

The questionnaire seemed to cover everything, and there was space for personal remarks and requests.

Ceil's eyes went on scanning the form. 'Ah, here we are,' she said. '*This* is what I'm looking for... "all information is accepted in good faith and we cannot be held responsible for incorrect information given."' She broke off and sighed. 'Well, there you have it, Miss Downing. All you have to do is to pull in your own clients, according to Mr Khaled.'

There was the sound of an approaching car and she glanced up. A moment later Jonathan was parking his car at the foot of the steps, then he opened the door and got out.

Ceil's heart lurched crazily, then she got up and went to the top of the wide, shallow steps.

'Hi. What a surprise!'

'How are things with you?' he asked. 'I'd begun to think I'd imagined Mombasa and decided it was time to look you up. I got your address from Tom.'

'That's nice.' She laughed a little and stood back, looking down at her crumpled shorts and grubby bare feet. 'I'm always busy—as you can see for yourself. I was going to contact you, actually, as soon as I got a bit more organised.'

'Are you sorry I came?' he mocked.

'No, not at all.' Ceil found herself wishing she didn't look such a freak. 'Since I have only myself to consider, I never know when to stop and call it a day. By the time I decide to have a bath and get into something decent, it always seems to be round about midnight. Except for going in to Nairobi when necessary, I've just about forgotten how to dress properly.'

'Well, I hardly expected to find you wearing a little number glittering with rhinestone buttons, after all. In any case, you still manage to look beautiful.' He turned. 'So that's the tower? In other words, where you plan to work behind sun-warmed buttressed walls?'

'I'll show you around later, but I really must change, Jonathan. I'm feeling awful.'

She went to the table, and lifted the questionnaires and began to tap them into place. 'I've been glancing through some work which was sent to me by Abdel Khaled. He doesn't waste much time! A desk, computer and office equipment were delivered here before I'd even moved in. They've all been shoved into one of the bedrooms, until I decide what to do and something is done about the tower.'

As she busied herself with the questionnaires, she was aware of Jonathan's eyes taking in everything. After a moment he said, 'You mentioned just now that you only have yourself to consider. Am I to take that to mean that you're living here on your own?'

She lifted her long lashes and her eyes locked with his. 'Yes.'

'I thought *he* was—moving in with you? What went wrong?'

'Nothing went wrong, since he doesn't exist, except in your imagination. I have a romantic commitment with a house, not a man.'

He laughed very softly. 'My, my—and so we could have ended up being romantically reckless in Mombasa after all? What a waste of that moon over the shivering waters!'

'I'm not that reckless.' Her voice had an edge to it.

'I don't go along with that, Ceil. I should say you're very reckless—coming to Africa to take up residence in a house which borders a wild-life park.'

'I must confess, Jonathan, I didn't know that until after I arrived here and Tom pointed it out to me, but it would have made no difference to me. Not once have I considered selling the house. My being alone here is self-inflicted. You know, your presumptuousness in leaping to conclusions really angered me.'

'Is that why you didn't correct me?' he asked.

'It is, yes, but one of my rules happens to be—I offer information about myself only when I think it necessary.' As she looked at him, she tried to appear offhand.

His eyes held hers. 'And you didn't think it necessary to tell me that *he* doesn't exist?'

'It didn't seem important. After all, we merely happened to spend some time together in Mombasa—and now, may I get you a cold drink? After that I'd like to change. You can sit out here and admire the garden.' She laughed. 'Isn't it a mess?'

'I came out here to see you, not the garden, although it looks OK to me. I wanted to see how things were going with you.'

His eyes went to the questionnaires. They were now in a neat pile on the wicker table which, along with four matching chairs, Ceil had discovered in a small storage-room in the garden.

'It would appear that you've started work?' Jonathan sounded curious.

'Oh, these? Well, yes. Abdel sent me some question-naires, so that I could get started.'

'Tell me, Ceil, have you any idea what you're be-coming involved in?' His tone was not encouraging.

Looking at him in exasperation, she said, 'Well, of course I know. What makes you so suspicious?'

He shrugged. 'There's a lot about this set-up which puzzles me. For one thing, how is it you're working from home for a company based in Mombasa? Why don't these people have a branch in Nairobi?'

'I'm that branch now. Look,' she lifted her hands and dropped them again, 'it's not the kind of work I'd like to boast about, although it's all right, but working from home is going to suit me very well. I'll be able to supervise the alterations to my house and to plan and work on the interior. That's only one of the benefits I have going for me, by having my office right here. Don't you see, Jonathan?'

She began to gather the questionnaires together, then she waved them in front of him and laughed.

'I'll tell you about these one day—I promise. You might even want to become one of my clients.'

'Don't bank on it.' He turned to look at the garden. 'And so you live in this faded pink fortress all on your own?'

'What a disappointment it must be to you to find out that after all I'm not living with some guy, Jonathan!' She was beginning to feel angry.

He turned back to look at her. 'Let me give you a little advice, Ceil—not that I expect you to listen. This is no place for a girl to be living on her own.'

'How do you know?' She stared at him with ill-concealed hostility.

'For the simple reason that I happen to read the crime statistics.'

'Don't be a bore!' she said.

'I'm not being a bore. I'm being realistic.'

She wanted to hit back at him for making her feel threatened. 'Realistic? What was being realistic about driving out here today, when you thought I was living with someone? You could have put paid to my—affair. I was going to call you, remember? Not only that, but now you start criticising my work. What do you know about it, anyway?'

'The point is—what do *you* know about it? What is this information Abdel Khaled is so anxious to get hold of, anyway?' demanded Jonathan.

'I'll tell you all about it one day. First, I have to get the tower organised to accommodate my office equipment. When I'm totally organised, you'll be the first to know what it's all about. Now, make yourself comfortable and I'll be with you in a few minutes.' She picked up the questionnaires.

When she returned, she was carrying a tray with two long glasses of orange juice. Jonathan was leaning against one of the white pillars, surveying the garden, and as he turned to look at her his eyes went over her white trousers and the black top which had narrow shoulder straps. Before changing, she had taken a quick shower, and since her hair was damp she had taken it back and fastened it with a clasp. She looked golden and beautiful, and her new tan drew attention to her green eyes and ash-blonde hair.

Setting the tray down, she said, 'Don't you just love this house? Even though you're an architect?'

'What do you mean? Even though I'm an architect?' He sounded amused. 'What difference does that make?'

'It makes a lot of difference, I should imagine. There are a number of reasons why you should find something wrong with it.'

'I come across these old houses all the time. I'm living in one at the moment, and am in the process of buying— and renovating—another.'

'But, being an architect, you'll obviously see a lot wrong with them, let's face it. After all, they're old— but this one does have nice big windows, lots of french doors, and large and sunny rooms going for it, even though it's not factor-planned.'

'What do you know about a house being factor-planned?' His smile deepened. 'In any case, I'll decide after I've seen over it.'

'I can see you're going to give me a bad time.' Ceil finished her drink and stood up. Let's have a look round and then you can tell me what you think of everything. I'd like you to stay for lunch. Will you? It will just be a case of last night's left-over sausage pie, potato salad, and there's cheese and fresh fruit. I'd *like* you to stay.'

'That sounds great.' He smiled that particular smile which she was beginning to know so well now.

He seemed impressed by the house, she noticed, as she showed him around.

'Sometimes,' she said, 'I find myself going from one task to another. There's so much to do here. I've been editing—all those letters over there, and photographs. But the big moment has come. I'll get the key to the tower.'

After she had got it, they went down the steps and walked the short distance to the tower, which was to one side of the lounge and overlooked the pool and pool-house.

'I was a little nervous of this spiralling iron staircase at first.' She paused for a moment and looked down at Jonathan, who was following. 'You know, I hate to think of my poor aunt, alone here, during that particular time in history.'

Jonathan kept his eyes on her face. 'She could have left. From what I've heard, many people living on farms or in lonely areas locked their houses, hoped for the best and headed for some place else—in some instances, Nairobi. Your great-aunt appears to have been as reckless and as unpredictable as you are.'

Ceil turned away impatiently and began to climb the stairs again.

'Don't you admire reckless women—just a little?' she asked him. They had reached the top of the tower and she turned to look at him.

'Reckless women are like fluttering moths—foolishly attracted to danger,' he told her.

'Really? And what about reckless men?'

'Reckless men, Ceil, are too smart to end up getting singed. They usually get what they want without landing in trouble.'

Without stopping to think she said, 'Is that why you were so reckless in Mombasa? You mentioned that we could have ended up being romantically reckless, after all, and yet——'

His blue eyes seemed to darken as he cut in, 'OK, Ceil, what's all this about?' The balance between them had been subtly altered and she was immediately aware of the exciting sexual undercurrent between them. 'Are you trying to bait me again?'

'Of course I'm not trying to bait you! I'm only teasing.'

'Teasing?' His eyes held hers.

'Yes, teasing.'

'Well, come here. I'll show you what teasing is all about.'

Suddenly he reached for her and pulled her towards him. Her breasts were crushed against his hard chest. When he kissed her she struggled to get her feelings under control. After a moment, however, she managed to pull herself together and pushed him away.

'That wasn't necessary, was it?'

'Maybe not, but it reflects my attitude towards—teasing.'

Her green eyes were beginning to glitter.

'Teasing means one thing to me—like honesty—and apparently something quite different to you.'

Jonathan shrugged his shoulders. 'How about getting back to business? Which was the object of coming up here, after all. Think twice before you tease.'

'I don't know why you had to do that, Jonathan. It *wasn't* necessary!'

'Maybe just to humour you,' he mocked. 'Look, when you have a rough idea of what it is you want here, I'll draw up a plan for you, since you seem hell-bent on staying on in your fortress and using this tower as your office.'

Flooding with anger at his callousness, she snapped, 'Just to humour me? I don't happen to appreciate that remark.'

'In that case, let me change it. Teasing happens to excite men to passionate behaviour, or didn't you know? Is that better?'

'No, it isn't. I'm beginning to have second thoughts about everything—including you. Maybe I should get someone else to draw the plans.'

He came over to her. 'What did you expect just now? Naturally I was conscious of your taunt.' His eyes went over her. 'I only did what I understood was expected of me, after all.'

'You're a typical man!' she flamed. 'Whenever the opportunity seems to present itself, you immediately set about trying to establish something physical!'

'Think about what I've said. Teasing excites a guy to passionate behaviour.' His eyes challenged her. 'But, to change the subject, I can put you on to a reliable handyman. He's worked for me and I've always been very satisfied.'

Ceil's lovely face still had a haughty, angry look. 'Well, I *do* have to have help, after all.'

A few minutes later she found herself responding to some of Jonathan's suggestions about joining the tower to the house and making certain changes within the tower.

At lunchtime he watched her, with slightly narrowed eyes, as she transferred food and dishes from a trolley to the round wicker table, which was covered with a cloth the colour of an ink-blue hydrangea. Fully aware of the way in which he was looking at her, Ceil found herself thinking that he seemed to think he had some sort of claim on her.

'Well, how's it been, living next to a game park?' he asked. 'You still haven't told me.'

'It's very convenient, actually. The animals don't pop over to borrow an egg or a cup of sugar.'

'Aren't you lonely?' he asked.

'I'm too busy to be lonely.'

'Scared?'

'There's no need to mock. Why should I be scared?'

'I'm not mocking—I'm serious. After all, where you come from there are no animal noises in the night— unless you lived next to the zoo? Did you?'

'No, I didn't.' Suddenly she laughed. 'You know, I shouldn't be telling you this, but I *do* have the feeling of being watched sometimes, and the air often seems to smell of animals. I keep telling myself I'm just being silly.' She sat back in her chair and met his eyes. 'Why do people have these destructive forces to plague them from time to time? And by the way, please don't ever kiss me again.'

'In other words you're nervous living next door to wild animals? And—by the way—I can't promise.' His eyes went to her lips. 'Especially when I'm tantalised.'

'"In other words", I didn't say I was nervous.'

'But I'm saying if for you,' he said quietly.

'Well, don't, Jonathan. To take up where I left off, though—if we're to work together as architect and client, let's not have another scene like the one that took place in the tower before lunch. It was totally uncalled-for.'

'I think you only got what you deserved.' He had finished his lunch and, pushing his chair back from the table, he swung his leg over the arm and lifted his glass to his lips. He moved lithely, like a cat, she thought.

'You haven't told me about *your* house,' she said.

He thought for a moment. 'I bought it as an investment. I've done that twice before—bought a house, made structural improvements and then sold, at a profit. On both occasions I've lived in the house and then moved on, and, since I have a buyer for this present house, that's what I'll be doing again.' He laughed. 'I have a buyer—with complications. His wife wants me to sell the house fully furnished, and that includes all the curtains. So I'll be left destitute—unless, of course, someone takes pity on me.'

'If you're hinting—the answer is no.' In spite of herself, however, Ceil was excited. 'Besides, you don't like my house.'

'I said I don't like the idea of you living alone in it. I do have the option on a charming old house, with a lot going for it, but it wouldn't be a bad idea for you to come and see the one I'm in, actually. You might get a few ideas, when it comes to changes here.'

'I'd like that. There's a phone in this house which is disconnected, but Tom is arranging for it to be connected, so I'll ring you. Otherwise, Jonathan, I'll pop into your office when I'm next in Nairobi to collect my post. So you can see that I'm always busy here and there's no time to feel nervous. I end up going to bed so late that there's virtually no time to brood on those mysterious noises.'

'What mysterious noises?'

She realised at once that she had played into his hands.

'Well, the tin—I mean corrugated iron—roof cracking, for one.' She laughed lightly. 'What is it you want to hear? That I hear all sorts of animal noises, and that they all sound close enough to be on my own property?'

Jonathan changed his position and stretched his legs out in front of him. 'Perhaps you should think of sharing your house?' He lifted his arms and linked his fingers behind his head.

'In other words, I need a big strong man to share the house?'

'How did you guess?' His eyes held hers. 'As soon as I've sold the house, I'll share your house with you—on a strict business basis, of course. It makes sense.'

'To you, maybe,' she retorted. 'I hardly know you, after all.'

However, she knew he was right. He could stay here until she got used to living in Africa, where her nearest neighbours just happened to be wild animals. 'I'll have to think about it.' Her voice was taut and offhand. 'But if I approve, I must make it plain that I wouldn't tolerate any interference in my private life.'

'That, believe it or not, cuts both ways.' Jonathan stood up and looked down at her. 'Surely that goes without saying?'

'Well, yes, of course. I can let you have my two guest-rooms and, of course, your own bathroom. You'll naturally have the run of the house.'

'Very much, if fact, like a good watchdog?' he mocked.

She watched him as he reached for his jacket and slung it across his shoulder. 'Thank you for the lunch.' His eyes held hers. 'As much as I'd like to stay, I have to get back to the office.'

A few moments later Ceil watched his car as he drove through the big black wrought-iron gates, which he had left open. He got out of the car and shut them, then he waved.

Waving back at him, she felt a sudden sense of loss. For the first time since moving into the house, she knew the black depression of being alone.

CHAPTER SIX

SATISFIED with the work she had done in the house, Ceil had relaxed in a bath. She had also taken her time washing her hair and applying nail-polish.

Reaching for the voluminous white caftan which she had bought in Mombasa, she slipped it over her head and the folds fell to the floor and floated about her as she walked about the room. For good measure, she decided to wear her heavy gold necklace and her ankle-strap sandals.

She had just poured herself a glass of perfectly chilled wine when she heard a car arriving and, going out to the veranda, saw Jonathan coming towards the steps. She was immediately aware of the excitement he created in her. At that moment nothing else mattered but to see him there.

'What are you doing here?' she called out.

Taking the last two steps at one time, he said, 'That's not a very nice way to greet a visitor who's come straight from an exhausting day at the office to see you!'

She laughed. 'How nice to see you, Jonathan. There, is that better?' Her eyes went to the two envelopes he was carrying and then he held them out to her.

'Miss Downing, may I, as the sun goes down, present my credentials? There they are, as requested by you—a letter from your lawyer, Mr Thomas Mzima, and one from my bank manager, Mr Samuel Sabaki—otherwise better known as Mr Pessimistic Sabaki.'

'And, I suppose, with good reason,' laughed Ceil. 'By the way, you're just in time for a glass of wine. Do come through to the drawing-room. The upholsterers are coming tomorrow,' she added, 'and I'm so excited! It might have been the logical thing to wait to decorate the room before I had the upholsterers come along, but I want to start enjoying the house now,' she told him.

His blue eyes met hers and his look was appreciative. 'Are you going out?' he asked.

'No.' She stood back. 'This is the Arab caftan I bought in Mombasa, as a matter of fact. This is the first time I've worn it, actually. To get back to the painters and the upholsterers, though. I'll just have to keep moving everything from room to room, won't I? It's as simple as that. Obviously, Mr Caister, in many respects, you don't appear to know very much about women.'

His intensely blue eyes went over her. 'Just how much I *do* know about women, Miss Downing, I'll leave you to find out for yourself.'

His teasing amused her one moment and irritated her the next. Her green eyes were beginning to glitter. 'I think we'd better change the subject,' she said. 'Make yourself comfortable while I go and pour you some wine.'

When she returned from the kitchen, she was carrying an opened bottle of chilled wine and one glittering glass, which had a very long rose-pink stem.

As she poured wine into the glass, Jonathan said, 'Where's yours?'

'Over there.' She smiled as she passed him the glass and tried not to permit the thrill of their fingers touching to go to her head. Moving away from him, she picked up her glass, which matched his.

'Well, Jonathan, here's to your credentials. They'd better be good.'

He raised his glass. 'To prove how confident I am, and since you're not going out, I'd like to take you to dinner.'

'Where would we go?' she asked.

'Well, since I couldn't ring you, I went ahead and booked a table at a private game ranch.'

'It sounds exciting,' Ceil said. 'I'd like that.'

'Are you afraid of cheetahs?' She saw the mockery in his expression. 'The owners have two pet cheetahs who like to mingle with the guests.'

Ceil shrugged. 'It will be an experience. Just as long as they don't start to chase me in this flowing garment!'

Later, as Jonathan parked the car at the ranch, he said, 'Are you ready to meet the cheetahs? I'll hold your hand if you like.'

'Maybe you should.'

The cheetahs seemed to stare right through the guests, and Ceil found herself tensing as the magnificent pair came near her.

'Somehow I thought they'd be asleep,' she said.

Jonathan laughed softly and took her hand.

On arrival, he had introduced her to the owners who, being very busy, soon disappeared, and to Don Pearson, one of the game rangers, who had joined them on the long lawn-level veranda before going through to the restaurant for dinner.

Obviously attracted to Ceil, Don was going to some length to explain that, contrary to common belief, cheetahs were of the dog family and not, in fact, cats.

'What's more,' he added, 'they're not man-eaters.'

'I can't tell you how relieved I am to hear that!' Ceil laughed shakily, as the animals came round to her chair again.

'On the other hand,' mocked Jonathan, 'they can be dangerous when they sense fear—*and* especially if it happens to be past their bedtime.'

'Oh, come off it, Jonathan!' Don showed his disapproval. 'Don't scare her. She's just out from England, after all.' He stood up and looked down at Ceil. 'Come and let me show you something. We'll be back in a minute.' He glanced at Jonathan.

Jonathan's blue eyes were unfathomable as he looked at Ceil.

Her feelings were unsettled as she went with Don to see what turned out to be a tiny hyena. Don explained that the small animal had been found by the owners as they were driving back from Mount Kenya. 'They'll be sending it to the animal orphanage soon, where it will be released into the park at a later stage.'

'In that case, it will be my neighbour,' she answered, as she admired the hyena.

'I was surprised to hear that you're living in Miss Downing's house, actually,' said Don. 'I didn't know the old lady, of course, but from what I've heard, she was quite a character in her day. But tell me, aren't you lonely there? Coming from England and all that...?'

Ceil straightened and shrugged her shoulders. 'Oh, I'm getting used to it, and I love the house, of course. Well,

I suppose we'd better be getting back to Jonathan. Thank you for showing me the orphan, Don.'

'I'd like to show you around the ranch one day, Ceil. This shouldn't make any difference to Jonathan, should it? I mean,' Don laughed a little, 'not with Xenia in the picture.'

His remark seemed calculated to let her know that there was a girl in Jonathan's life, she thought resentfully.

'I'd like to see over the ranch,' she said. 'Thank you.'

'I'll ring you,' he told her.

'You might have to keep trying, until the phone is connected,' she told him.

As they came back to the veranda, Jonathan stood up and his eyes met Ceil's. 'Well, ready to eat?' he asked.

'Yes—I'm starving!' She spoke lightly, but she was thinking of Don's remark. Why should she feel so ruffled? she asked herself.

She knew the answer, though. Like an idiot, she had fallen in love with Jonathan but, with the unusual name Xenia at the back of everything, this should help her to remain indifferent to Jonathan's charm.

'I'll drop over,' Don was saying, 'and we can make a plan about that day in the open, Ceil.'

'I'll look forward to it.' Her smile was totally false.

On the way in to the restaurant Jonathan said lightly enough, but she was aware of the touch of sarcasm, 'Well, the game ranger hasn't lost much time.'

After they had ordered, Ceil sat back and gazed about the vast, lantern-lit room with its high thatched roof and crossbeams. Overhead, white-bladed fans turned lethargically but, nevertheless, efficiently stirred the air.

Across the table from her, Jonathan exuded confidence. Tall, dark-haired, blue-eyed, tanned and nonchalant in a light oatmeal-coloured suit, he had turned the head of just about every woman in the large room. Looking at him, Ceil felt a sense of tremendous inner tension, as she realised that she was becoming more and more attracted to him.

His eyes met hers. 'What are you thinking about?' he asked.

'Nothing, really. I just feel so lucky. I can't believe I'm in Africa.'

'You're a long way from home, let's face it.' He went on holding her eyes. 'Apart from family, was there anyone you left behind?'

His question took her by surprise and she decided to play it cool.

'A boyfriend, you mean?' Her eyes mocked him.

'Yes—a boyfriend.'

'What is it you want to know? Besides, what difference does it make? You have your girlfriends, right?'

'It makes a lot of difference,' he said. 'Do you intend letting your parents and your—boyfriend—know that I'll be sharing the house with you?'

'Of course I intend letting my folks know.' Her voice was abrupt.

'You haven't answered my question.'

'I think I have. Besides, we're not really sure, at this stage, whether you *will* be sharing the house. I have to think about it very seriously. It's not just—it's not something one just flies into.' Ceil shrugged. 'I mean...'

He laughed softly. 'You sound flustered. Why?'

'I'm not. While we're on the subject, though, are you trying to link me to some guy in England so that it will make explaining easier on your side? I'm referring to a woman, of course, and I don't particularly mean your mother.'

Jonathan sat back and mocked her with his eyes. 'Ceil, I'm past the age when I have to explain anything to anybody. If it will put your mind at rest, however, I had something going with a girl, but we broke up three months ago. I still see Xenia, but, whatever it was, it's over.'

'Well, that's very convenient for you, isn't it?' Ceil glanced away. 'Especially as it seems to mean so little to you.'

At that moment, their food arrived, and then the wine. When it was served, Jonathan lifted his glass and stared at Ceil across the lantern-lit table with those exciting blue eyes.

'I can see you underestimate me,' he said. 'I've never wanted to feel tied down. In other words, there's no explaining to do.'

'Maybe it was something that needed clearing up, Jonathan, both on my part and yours. In other words...' she laughed a little '...there's no one important enough in *my* life to hurt.'

'Let's drink to that.' He raised his glass.

They were both quiet, going back in the car. Ceil asked Jonathan in for coffee, but he declined.

'I have an early start for Mombasa tomorrow,' he explained.

'Mombasa again?' She found herself wishing she were going with him.

'I have some odds and ends to tie up with the Italian I was telling you about. And so tomorrow, at the crack of dawn, you'll have the upholsterers on your doorstep?' he added.

'Yes. Next time you come here, you won't know the lounge. I think it's going to look quite beautiful.'

She found herself standing very close to him and wondered whether she would be making a terrible mistake by agreeing to have him here and whether she would end up going to bed with him. 'I'll get back to you.' Her voice exuded a nonchalance she did not feel. 'About sharing the house. I have to think about it seriously.'

'I don't like the thought of you living here on your own,' he said. 'For that matter, Ceil, I wouldn't like Xenia—or any other girl——living here. It's as simple as that. Think about what I've said. Goodnight.'

'Goodnight, and—thank you for dinner.'

He made no attempt to touch her, but somehow, Ceil had the feeling that was on purpose. He was too clever to touch her at this stage.

The upholsterers took four days to re-cover the giant wicker sofas and four matching chairs. During this time Ceil found herself wishing that Abdel Khaled had not sent her work before she had even planned her advertising campaign.

Torn between following the progress of the upholsterers and working in the garden-room, which was now serving as her temporary office, she was beginning to feel the strain. Added to this strain were her almost sleepless nights when, at the slightest creak in the house, her imagination ran wild.

Her mind was only half on what she was doing each time she got behind the computer. She found herself smothering one yawn after another and she longed to be attending to her own affairs. Often she was tempted to stop and make her way into another part of the house, where she always found something more interesting to do. Eventually, as guilt got the better of her, she would go back to her office and try to pick up where she had left off. It took all the will-power she had to carry on until a reasonable period had elapsed and she could think of closing down the system and finish work.

At the end of those four days, she was able to stand back and gaze at the transformation in her lounge. What a stroke of luck that she had been able to get the pink and shoot-green striped material for the cushions! She had visualised the colours from the start. In addition, dusty pink and delicate green pillows were piled high on the sofas and chairs.

Mainly to keep herself busy and her mind off the creaking and animal noises, which often seemed to be very close, she had worked late into the nights. As a result, she had completely restored a six-panel Japanese screen, which the upholsterers had fixed to the wall above one long sofa. She had also re-covered two lampshades which went on top of bases resembling Egyptian urns.

The upholsterers had gone. The telephone was connected and peace settled over the house, until a stray blue-eyed Siamese cat—from only heaven knew where—walked into the house, and into her life. He decided to stay, and she decided to name him Frank, after Ol' Blue Eyes—Frank Sinatra.

Piles of books were now scattered about in the dining-room, along with the many objects, some of them quite useless, which her great-aunt had obviously gathered on her travels in her palmy days. Old photographs had to be edited, which only added to the confusion. Curtains which had been taken down, to make way for new curtains which had been made by the upholsterers, were heaped all over the place. At the back of it all were the questionnaires.

Ceil had phoned Abdel Khaled to let him know that her telephone had now been connected, should he wish to get in touch with her. In turn, he went to some lengths to tell her to look after the computer. He mentioned this, he explained, in case there should be children visiting her house.

'There is a lack of reliable local facilities for repairs and maintenance of equipment, Miss Downing. I'm sure you will understand. Maintenance is also expensive and is becoming an increasing problem.'

It was strange, Ceil found herself thinking, that he should quibble about the high cost of maintenance when the government tax on computing equipment made purchase in Kenya prohibitive. So Tom had said, anyway, during a casual conversation.

She struggled to compile the advertisement which was to start her in business. It was to appear in a newspaper and in a magazine called *Catch Up*. She had decided to use her second name—Grace—in the ads, and give her box-number. But everything she wrote seemed ridiculous.

Let our computer find your perfect match. In
fact, we're so confident about finding you a
partner that we ask you to contact us right away.
In Mombasa, we already have hundreds of
members on our books whom we have matched
with care and understanding. These include
professionals and executives. We have had many
weddings to prove it. We are now offering this
unique service to Nairobi—and so, for an exciting and thrilling new future, phone or write to
Grace. In turn, we will forward you our information brochure. We will introduce you to
people. People change lives.

Outside, the sun shone, and she longed to be in it.
She started again.

While some dream of finding the right person,
others do it by contacting us. Someone waits for
you...

Eventually she got it together and heaved a huge sigh
of relief.

On the day she decided to go into Nairobi to place the
advertisement, she wondered what to do with Frank.
Realising the damage he could do to the new cushions,
she decided to shut him in the kitchen, and laughed outright as he gave her an outraged blue-eyed stare.

In town, she visited Tom Mzima's offices and then,
leaving her car parked outside, walked to the newspaper
and magazine offices. Afterwards, she did a little
shopping and had lunch before she went to see Jonathan
at his office.

Looking even more handsome than she remembered him, he got up from behind his desk.

'This is a pleasant surprise,' he greeted her. 'As a matter of fact, I was coming to see you tonight. I have the rough plans for the tower for you.'

'Oh, thank you! I can hardly wait to see them. By the way, I should have let you know, my phone has now been connected. I'll let you have the number right this minute.'

'Would you like a cup of coffee?' he asked, after she had written it down for him.

'No, thank you—I've just had lunch. I had to come into town on business.' She laughed. 'By the way, your credentials finally have my approval, so when you've completed the sale of your house, you can move in to Mnarani.'

'The sale has gone through,' Jonathan told her. 'Actually, I wanted you to see the house. Because it happens to be a house similar, in a way, to your own, you'd possibly be interested.'

'I would be. I *am* interested.'

'I hand over the keys to these people on Thursday.' He glanced at his watch. 'What about going out to see it now, before you drive back home?'

'That would be nice.' She smiled at him and then decided to tell him. 'I might as well put you into the picture, Jonathan. I've already started work—and I've had a stroke of luck. I've just come from Tom's office, and he's suggested that I might care to employ the son of the man who used to work for my aunt. Tom has actually gone so far as to speak to him, and he's willing to take over my garden and any odd jobs I have on hand. Everything seems to be falling into pattern.'

'How is it you've already started work before your advert has even appeared?' Jonathan asked.

'Well, I'm responsible for starting this agency—whatever—in Nairobi, but Abdel Khaled sent me work in advance, just to get me going.' She lifted her shoulders and dropped them. 'You might as well know everything, Jonathan. I'm going to be responsible for a section of Computer Rewards known as Computa-mate, which speaks for itself, I should imagine.'

She felt the full force of his blue eyes.

'What? You must be joking!' he exclaimed.

'I'm not joking. Why should I be joking?' Suddenly Ceil felt an unbearable impatience. Who did he think he was, anyway? 'Don't make fun of this, Jonathan. I'm not in the mood.'

'I just don't get it. Don't be so naïve! Let's be practical here. You don't know anything about these individuals in Mombasa. They might be quite corrupt. Sometimes, Ceil, you remind me of a blundering moth. Surely you must have some vague idea of the dangers?'

'Oh, what rubbish! I know enough. After all, I had quite a lengthy interview in Mombasa. This is going to be the kind of work I'll be doing, and it happens to be my business and nobody else's. I find I don't want to discuss it with you, after all.'

Jonathan went on staring at her with a concentration that angered her.

'Taking it at face value, you'd be arranging romances?' he demanded.

Ceil did not answer. Instead, she opened her bag and began to look for her car key.

'Ceil? I asked you a question.'

'Yes, I will be arranging romances. Why are you being so caustic?'

'Because I think you're an idiot. There's a difference between falling in love and a computer print-out.'

'What do you know about love?' she asked furiously. 'What is it *you* say when a new affair begins? We "had something going", but "whatever it was" is over? Is that love? Probably the computer has a lot going for it. The people concerned genuinely——'

He cut in, 'We're not talking about me, we're talking——'

'I don't *want* to talk, Jonathan! Just forget it!' She swung the key on the key-holder and asked herself why she had taken it out of her bag when her car was parked outside Tom's office and she still had to walk there.

'Well, you should talk about it. In times to come, you might well have to live with the knowledge that you've been responsible, one way or another, for a lot of misery and unhappiness—just because two names came up on a computer.'

Her outrage turned to incredulity.

'Such sensitivity! Besides, no one can guarantee results. It mentions that on our questionnaire——'

Jonathan laughed outright. 'On our questionnaire? When it comes to sensitivity, Ceil, perhaps you should begin to ask yourself a few questions!'

The sarcasm in his voice infuriated her. 'Perhaps *you*— look, don't use that tone with me, Jonathan. *If* you don't mind. I don't have to ask myself anything. I don't have to explain anything. The money Computa-mate is going to earn me will show society's appreciation of our work.'

'A certain sector of society, don't you mean? I credited you with more sense. What type of person would be bothered to pay for a service like that, unless there was something else behind it, of course?'

'Don't be so vile! There's nothing behind it. It simply means that many people are in fact prepared to pay because we will, in the long run, have provided them with what they need. Mombasa has already proved that, and what could be more moral and sensitive than that?'

'And so you call selling your soul to a computer moral and sensitive?' He shrugged. 'If you want to believe you're saving the nation, go ahead. You surprise me.'

'I don't care whether I surprise you or not!' Ceil stormed out to a scene of yellow sunlight and blue sky and made her way to where her car was parked.

Jonathan phoned soon after she got home.

'My first incoming call.' Her voice was stiff with sarcasm. 'And what a let-down! What do you want?'

'I want you to find me a mate. What else?'

She heard him laugh. 'Will you take down my particulars, or shall I fill in one of your questionnaires, which I understand, you'll let me have for a fee?'

She slammed the phone down, and when it rang again and kept ringing and ringing she answered only through sheer frustration. 'How long do you intend to keep this up?' she demanded. 'Don't waste my time!'

'Why are you so angry?' he asked. 'Does the truth hurt?'

'I don't like you, Jonathan. Do you know that?'

'I wouldn't bet on that, but, on the other hand, that could be in your own interests—and mine, of course—when I move in. It will help to keep things nice and businesslike.' She heard the blatant mockery in his voice.

'I don't want you moving in here. Will you get off my line?'

'For economic reasons, not to mention the fact that you're nervous at night, you need someone to share your house with you—and, for better or for worse, Ceil Downing, it might as well be me, right? You at least know me... Tom knows me...'

'I have no recollection of having said I'm nervous here,' she retorted. 'I made a joke about creaking and animal noises...'

'You've approved of my credentials. When can I move in? I'm being serious now.'

Ceil found herself wrestling with herself. Another long, lonely night reared its ugly head.

'As soon as you like.' She had resisted the temptation to cut off her nose to spite her face, but, nevertheless, she felt she had lost control of the situation. 'I'm in the middle of something—I have company.' She glanced down at Frank, who was sharpening his claws on the long leg of a rosewood table.

'Male or female?' Jonathan asked.

'Male. So, as you can see, my life has become both full and busy. I don't need you in it, except for econ-omical reasons—and, by the way, I shall expect your contribution towards rent and running this home on the first day of every month. Please bear that in mind—twenty-four hours a day.'

'Fine. I have a strict code when it comes to money matters. While we're on the subject of a full and busy life, might I remind you, Miss Downing, that that cuts two ways? My life is also full and busy.'

As she replaced the receiver Ceil was suddenly aware of the depression this piece of suggestive news had produced in her.

It was stupid to feel jealous. She knew that.

CHAPTER SEVEN

WHEN Don Pearson phoned to ask whether she would like to visit the game ranch on the same day as Jonathan was to move in, Ceil thought, why not? It would be a way to prove that her life was full and busy and a way to remind herself of Xenia and of Jonathan's remark about the fullness of *his* life.

Since Don had said he would pick her up in the morning and that, after driving out to view game, they would lunch at the restaurant at the ranch, she knew she would be back at Mnarani before Jonathan turned up, soon after five o'clock. What could be more convenient than for him to arrive to find Don sitting on her veranda enjoying a drink?

She decided to be frank with Don. 'I'd love that, but I'll have to be back before five. You see, for financial reasons, I'm going to have to share my house with someone, and that someone happens to be Jonathan Caister. Jonathan has, very conveniently for me, I must say, just sold his house and most of his furniture and curtains, so moving in here for a while will help solve some of *his* problems as well as my own.'

'I see.' Don spoke with a hint of disappointment in his voice. 'I'm surprised you speak of financial reasons, though. I understood your great-aunt had left you a substantial amount of money—along with the house, that is.'

Ceil felt a spurt of anger. 'Really? What an amazing rumour!'

Don flushed. 'It's just that I'm surprised to hear that Jonathan will be sharing your house. It could lead to quite a bit of ill feeling with Xenia.'

After he had rung off, Ceil replaced the receiver and sat staring at nothing in particular.

Later in the morning, Don picked her up in his car and drove to the ranch, where they transferred to an open Land-Rover and then drove out to view game.

Afterwards they had lunch on the long veranda with its wide thatch overhang and low, split-pole railing which separated it from the sweeping lawns.

There were a number of guests present, and it was all exciting to Ceil, who was beginning to feel very much a part of Africa now.

Just as she had hoped, they were sitting on the veranda back at Mnarani when Jonathan arrived. Don had decided to accept a beer and Ceil had poured herself a light shandy, and she had arranged a few snacks on one of her great-aunt's silver platters.

Jonathan's incredibly blue eyes gave nothing away as, glancing carelessly in Don's direction, he said, 'How's it, Don? Hot enough for you?' He began to loosen his tie and then he looked at Ceil. 'Hi. You look as if you've spent time in the sun.' His eyes went over the purple polished cotton shirt she was wearing with khaki trousers.

'Don and I have been viewing game at the ranch and then we had a marvellous lunch on the veranda.' She crossed her trousered legs and began swinging one strappy sandal. 'Join us for a drink when you've settled in.'

Ignoring her invitation, he said, 'And so you're becoming quite used to the cheetahs?'

She laughed. 'Yes, but I can't say I really trust them, though.'

'Well, that's what Africa's all about. Wild animals, after all, are not to be trusted—no matter what the experts have to say on the matter.'

'Ha, ha!' Don interrupted. 'Is that getting at me, by any chance?'

'I said the experts,' Jonathan replied callously. He looked at Ceil. 'I'd like to dump my things, if I may?'

'Well, of course.' She leaned forward and put her glass on the table. 'Don, please excuse me for a few moments, while I show Jonathan where to go.'

Don half rose to his feet. 'Don't hurry. I don't mind waiting, unless you need a hand? Not that I'm an expert, of course.'

'You sit and enjoy your well-earned beer, Don. You don't have to be an expert to do that.' Jonathan, thought Ceil, was at his rudest.

She led the way to one of the two guestrooms, which she had partially cleared to accommodate any furniture which Jonathan had kept back from the sale and might wish to bring along.

After she had explained this to him he said, 'That was very civil of you, I'm sure. I'll be hiring a small truck tomorrow. Don't faint—it's not as bad as it sounds. I have a few bits and pieces—not much, but nothing my car can handle.'

'If I am fainting, it's because of your bad manners.' Ceil glanced around the room. 'Well, there's no reason why this furniture can't be moved out. I merely left fur-

niture in both rooms because you said you'd sold everything. There's a very nice store-room, actually. This is
a very adaptable house.'

'Just leave things as they are for the moment, and let's
hope the term adaptable will apply to the two people
who are going to live in it.'

Judging by his moody expression, Jonathan was
jealous, Ceil thought, but the thought did not bring her
any particular joy. She couldn't stop herself falling in
love with him, but she could stop herself becoming just
another name to him, after he'd made love to her. Just
as long as Don didn't get the wrong idea, having him
visit Mnarani was going to serve a purpose.

'Everything should work out, Jonathan,' she said.
'Just as long as you keep to your side of the fence and
I keep to mine, don't you think?'

'And you made sure Don Pearson was here to back
up your statement, right?'

She drew an impatient breath. 'Let's dispense with the
sarcasm, Jonathan. You should know, without my
having to say anything, that you're free to entertain here
and to——'

'Have somebody to visit *me*?' He spoke with sarcastic
mockery.

'And to stay, if you want.' Her eyes met his, challenging him. 'You know, a night here, a night there...'

'I see.' He looked at her with faint amusement. 'Let's
get this straight, Ceil. I have no sexual frustrations, so
that I need a night here and a night there. But don't let
me keep you from the ranger.'

Feeling suddenly absurdly excited that he was probably
jealous, Ceil went towards a chest of drawers and opened

the top drawer. 'I've had some keys cut for you.' She kept her voice very casual, just to aggravate him. 'This one is for the double garage, which we'll share, of course. This one is——'

Intense and vivid, his eyes met hers. 'Just drop them back in the drawer.' He was obviously irritated by the fact that he had placed himself in a situation where he was being handed the keys of a house which did not belong to him. Well, that was his problem, she thought.

Turning away from her, he left the room on his way back to his car and she stood for a moment, wondering whether she had done the right thing by having him here. With nerves that had started to jangle, she went back to the veranda. The sun was going down and it was getting cooler. Jonathan was busy at his car, which was parked near to Don's at the foot of the steps. Her eyes went to Don's practically empty glass beer mug. 'Don, do let me get you another beer.'

He glanced at his watch. 'I think I'd better be getting along—I've got work waiting for me at the ranch.' He finished what was left of his drink and stood up. 'Today's been great, Ceil.'

Ceil was conscious of Jonathan's sarcastic look as he passed them on his way to the french doors which led into the lounge.

'I enjoyed it, Don. Thank you for taking me.'

After he had gone, she took a deep, calming breath.

As Jonathan came back to the veranda he said, 'So, for Miss Ceil Downing, the throbbing drums of Africa are beginning to sound?'

He had, she noticed, changed into white linen trousers and a dark blue shirt. She watched him as he began to open a lager and pour it into a glass.

'You could say the drums are sounding.' Her voice was abrupt, as she picked up the sarcasm in his remark.

He lifted his lashes to look at her. 'By the way, I don't expect drinks on the house. I've brought my own supply. OK?'

Ceil shrugged. 'Do as you think best. Oh—I eat most of my meals out here on the veranda. You can eat wherever and whenever you like.'

Before he lifted his glass to his lips Jonathan laughed, but his eyes were impatient as they swept the veranda.

'The veranda suits me very well. I don't mind eating out here—unless, of course, you happen to be entertaining, which seems to be on the cards.'

'Well, you know what they say,' she answered with sarcastic sweetness, 'the more the merrier.'

After a moment he said, 'I see you have three tables here. Maybe I'll use that one over there, unless that's the one you use?' He turned to look at her through thick lashes.

This definitely has not been a good idea, she thought.

'Use that one, by all means, if it will please you. Why don't you put your car away—unless you're going out?'

'Why should I be going out?' he mocked. 'I've only just arrived.'

'I merely happen to be thinking about your dinner,' she snapped. 'I was wondering, since you haven't garaged your car, whether you were in a hurry to eat and whether you were, in fact, going to visit your girlfriend.'

He ignored that. 'I'll put it away later—and I'm in no hurry to eat—or do you call it *dine* out here?'

'*Dine* suits me very well, actually.' Ceil drew the last word out and gave him a haughty look.

'While we're on the subject of dining, you've been out most of the day, I should imagine. Probably this will form the pattern of things to come. I want you to know, therefore, that I don't expect you to rush back and cook, just because I happen to have moved in—not today, or any other day.' As Jonathan spoke, she was acutely aware of his physical presence, the lean strength of him, the male grace and elegance of him—and of his cheek!

'Meals are part of the deal,' she reminded him, with sweet sarcasm. 'It's no problem, since I happen to eat myself, to put up a meal for you too.'

After a moment he went on, 'There happens to be a lot more involved here than meals, Ceil. The main thing is that we feel comfortable together.'

'Oh, I agree.' As she drew the word out, the tone of her voice was baiting. 'Believe me, *I'm* trying.'

'I'm sure the preparing of meals is something we can work out—and share, as it so happens—without getting in one another's way...that is, if we're to enjoy a completely mature relationship. I'm merely a paying guest. At any rate, I'm not some prominent nature conservationist visiting a five-star game ranch.'

Ceil cut in with a temper she could not control, 'Some expert on animals, you mean? So what do you suggest we do, Jonathan? I'm mature enough, I believe, to want to put you at ease.'

Leisurely, he went to lean one shoulder against a white pillar. 'I appreciate that. Look, what I'm getting at is—

I don't want you to worry about me. My advice to you
is—treat me as someone who's sharing a house with you,
with meals if and when they come. We have to be very
clear about this.'

She lifted a hand and pushed her hair away from her
cheek. 'This is silly. Why are we going on like this?'

The sunset, which had been all pink, red and deep
gold, had completely faded and it was almost dark. Seven
ha-da-dahs, a kind of ibis, flew over the house and their
cries were weird and, this evening, mournful, Ceil
thought. She always made a point of counting them,
morning and evening. Sometimes there were seven.

Leaving Jonathan for a moment, she went to switch
on the lantern-shaped lights all along the veranda. When
she had done this she came back to him, their eyes met
and something like a high-voltage wire hissed and
crackled between them. Ceil heard herself draw a small
sharp breath, as the thrill of awareness shot through her.

She saw a muscle tighten in his cheek and the sudden
change in his eyes told her that he was as aware of her
as she was of him.

'I think it's pretty obvious—now that I'm actually
here, you're having an attack of nerves.' In contrast to
the brooding expression in his eyes, his voice was faintly
mocking. 'After all, I should imagine you're very inexperienced when it comes to keeping a boarding-house.'

'Oh, very funny! What am I supposed to do? Break
down laughing? You can be very sarcastic, Jonathan.
Very sarcastic and very confusing. I *am* inexperienced,
and if I am having an attack of nerves it's because
you——'

He cut in and his voice was impatient now. 'Make no mistake, if we continue like this, we'll end up disagreeing and disputing everything, which will make it impossible for this to work. *I* want it to work. Don't you?' His eyes held hers.

'Why is it important to you for it to work? After all, you're not totally reliant on me to provide a roof over your head.'

He laughed. 'No, I'm not, as it happens. One of the reasons, believe it or not, is that I don't like the idea of any girl living here alone. Does that answer your question? But now that Don Pearson has come into the picture, perhaps you feel you've made a mistake?'

'Don could move in tomorrow, actually.' Ceil wanted to fight back. 'After all, the house is big enough to accommodate the three of us. I could use the garden-room as a bedroom.'

'There's something you should know now—no matter how adaptable this house may be, if it's a commune you have in mind, count me out,' Jonathan told her.

'Why say these things, then? If you ask a stupid question, you can expect a stupid answer!'

'Come, don't be touchy, Ceil.'

'I can't help being touchy. You've seen to that.'

'When the situation is analysed, I guess I'm as touchy as you are,' he said. 'After all, I've never been expected to dance to the tune of a very beautiful landlady before.'

'Well, Mr Caister, there's a first time for everything, after all, but, in any case, you don't have to dance to my tune,' she reminded him.

He laughed. 'Take my word for it, Miss Downing, I'm not going to.'

Feeling angry and confused, Ceil went through to the lounge, where she turned on two lovely reading-lamps before making her way to the kitchen.

Jonathan lost no time in following her and, without looking at him, she said, 'This casserole will take about thirty minutes. I prepared it before I went out with Don this morning.'

'That's fine,' he answered. 'Would you like a sherry?'

She turned to look at his face to see how this remark was meant.

'Are you offering me a sherry?'

'Yes, I am offering you a sherry.'

'After what you said about not expecting drinks on the house?'

He leaned against one of the cabinets. 'Is that a no I'm hearing?'

'Yes, it's a no you're hearing. I will have a sherry, but it will be my own.'

He straightened. 'Let's put an end to the birth-pains, Ceil, and begin to count down. I'll pour you a sherry—my sherry. OK?'

She stared back at him. 'OK. To count down—a sherry would be nice. I'd like to feed Frank first, though. Frank happens to be a stray Siamese cat.'

'So we have a cat?' Jonathan laughed a little.

They ended up by taking their drinks out to the veranda, where conversation revolved about alterations to the tower and other parts of the house.

Later, Ceil set one of the tables and they even joked about it. Apart from the lanterns on the veranda, she had placed a fat candle in the centre of the table. Beyond the veranda, it was as black as velvet. In the distance, somewhere, an animal barked—probably a bush-buck, which had been disturbed—or a wild dog, which sent shivers down her spine.

'And so you've been eating out here every night on your own?' Jonathan's voice was accusing.

'Since I lived alone, yes, but always much earlier—before it got too dark and I started having visions of all sorts of wild animals staring at me from secret places in the garden. There are times when I ask myself what side of the fence the hyenas are on—my side or theirs!'

'And so you *were* nervous?'

Ceil lifted her shoulders. 'Not nervous—but naturally, having someone here is going to make a difference to my well-being.'

Jonathan sat back and looked at her across the flickering candle. 'You know, I found myself thinking about you.' He spoke with exasperated anger. 'I wondered how long it would be before you put your house on the market, but with you, I'm always finding things I don't expect.'

'You don't know me at all.' She kept her voice cool. 'After all, up until Mombasa you hadn't even known I existed.'

'But you do exist. Now that I'm here, perhaps I can begin to get down to some work at the office without any unsettling thoughts nagging at me. At least I know you're safe at night.'

'I suppose I should feel flattered.' Ceil spoke as lightly as she could. '*You* worry about me. *Tom* worries about me...'

'Well,' he stood up, 'you're a very remarkable girl—
in your own way, of course. I'll help you with these
dishes.'

As she said goodnight to him, she realised how vulnerable she was, for she found him attractive and—when
they were not arguing—interesting and amusing.

When she awoke it was morning and the house was
very quiet—it was obvious that Jonathan had gone to
his office in Nairobi. Feeling suddenly alert with appre-
hension, she turned over to look at the small clock on
the bedside table, and then she sat bolt upright. It was
ten o'clock. Ten o'clock! She had never slept as late as
this. It was also obvious that, since moving into the
house, last night had been the first night she had slept
soundlessly, which made her realise how badly she had
been sleeping here on her own.

Before going to prepare breakfast she went along to
Jonathan's rooms. He had, she noticed, made his bed,
but he had left damp towels on the floor. Strangely
enough, until just a few moments ago she had not considered who was going to tidy his part of the house, and
once again, she felt acutely embarrassed.

Amazingly enough, Tom Mzima solved this problem
for her, later in the day, by phoning to say that Saba
Kabaki was willing to start working for her immediately.
He would, of course, live on the property.

'Saba,' he went on, 'means seven in Swahili, in case
you're wondering. You see, Saba was born at seven on
the seventh day of the seventh month.'

'How interesting,' she answered. 'Tom, this is great
news. I just can't tell you. I've been wondering how to
handle this situation—you know, about Jonathan's part

of the house. I'd feel so awkward going in there every morning to tidy up—like a wife, almost.'

Tom chuckled. 'It is best you keep out of his rooms, Ceil. Knowing Jonathan, he would not want you tidying up after him. With your permission, then, I will drive Saba out to your house, so that you and he can reach an arrangement.'

'Oh, super—and, Tom, tell him I'd like him to come prepared to stay. It would fit in here very well.'

'I will do that—and he wishes me to convey to you that, apart from being an experienced gardener, he is experienced when it comes to taking care of laundry matters and so on.'

Later in the day, Tom's car came to a halt in front of the veranda steps, and Ceil's amused green eyes went to the bicycle which was fastened to the roof.

She liked Saba Kabaki immediately and, in turn, he was satisfied with the money she was prepared to pay and with his quarters—a small cottage.

'Life is so strange, Tom,' she said, after Saba had gone to the cottage with his belongings. 'I seem to be following in my great-aunt's footsteps.'

He laughed lightly. 'Let us hope you don't! From what I have heard, it would appear that your great-aunt did not enjoy a happy love-affair. We don't want this happening to you—not with Jonathan in the house.'

'It won't,' Ceil answered abruptly.

She walked with Tom to his car and then stood watching as he drove off.

* * *

The days slipped by. Jonathan seemed to be busy and was bringing work home, and Ceil did not see much of him.

The plans of the tower had been approved and the handyman and the painters arrived. In the midst of the noise, Ceil managed to sort through some of the items which had belonged to her great-aunt. She was amazed to come across embroidered silk lingerie from Italy which, although bought years ago, was still in the original wrappings. In turn, she was touched when she discovered a black velvet sombrero. Where had this been bought? Spain? And with whom—that mysterious man in her aunt's life?

As there was no postal delivery, Jonathan had offered to have her post box cleared every day in Nairobi, and, surprisingly enough, there were a number of requests for questionnaires and replies to the ones she had already sent out.

And finally, the lounge and dining-room were painted.

'I'm sorry things have been so chaotic around here,' Ceil said one night, as she and Jonathan were dining on the long veranda. 'You're lucky you've been away during the daytime. The noise has been an assault on the nerves! Still, you must be heartily sick of everything. The furniture gets put back tomorrow. I suppose you were right—I should have had the rooms painted first, before having the furniture re-covered, that is. I thought you were just being critical.'

Jonathan laughed, and she thought what a wonderful laugh he had—so warm and infectious.

'You live and learn. I speak from bitter experience.'

At that moment, Don Pearson chose to show up and as he parked his car Ceil got up and walked towards the steps.

'Hi!' she called out. 'You're just in time for a cup of coffee.'

Don had been making a nuisance of himself lately, but it suited her to have him in the picture.

When she turned round, Jonathan was already leaving the veranda and Saba had come out and was removing the dishes from the table.

As it happened, this pattern of things was nothing new. The moment Don appeared on the scene, if Jonathan happened to be there he would immediately leave, often without even bothering to greet Don.

Ceil was working in the garden-room several days later, when Jonathan surprised her by walking in. He was holding a glass of pure orange juice in his hand and he exuded good health.

Looking up from the ornate white rattan chair, she said, 'Well, well, this is a surprise...pleasant, I hope?'

'Why shouldn't it be pleasant?' He lifted his glass to his lips and went on looking at her.

'Well, I don't want to fight with you—but you've been very rude to Don recently. I often brood about it.'

With his free hand he combed his hair back from his forehead.

'I don't think I've been rude. In any case, Don doesn't come to see me.'

'What was it you wanted to see me about?' she asked.

'Nothing. I just wanted to see you. Why? Am I breaking one of your golden rules by coming in here?'

She shrugged. 'Well, yes, you are.'

'Rules are made to be broken, after all.' His dark blue eyes went to the computer. 'How are the potent magical powers going?'

'I'm very busy.' Ceil tried to keep the edge of annoyance out of her voice.

'So business isn't going downhill?' His soft, sarcastic laugh infuriated her. With glittering green eyes she watched him as he put his glass down on her desk.

'Far from it.' She knew she would have been better off just to let the subject drop, but she went on, 'I was saying to Don that the days simply fly past. For instance, today I started work late for the simple reason that I had so many other things to see to. I was helping Saba move the furniture around in the lounge when, by a stroke of luck, Don turned up. It was super having him there to help.'

With smug satisfaction she immediately noticed the blaze of hostility in Jonathan's blue eyes.

'I'm sure it was. Let's give Don a loud round of applause, shall we?' Slowly, and without making any sound, he clapped his hands.

Ceil hung on to her temper. 'What did you think of it, by the way? Don suggested moving the *armoire*...'

'I noticed it had been moved, on my way in. I don't like it there. I preferred it where it was—against the far wall.' There was a baiting quality to his voice now, as his eyes went over the gold, tobacco and brown striped shirt she was wearing with drawstring khaki trousers. Several gold chains, which she had bought at Selfridges just before she left for Kenya, gleamed against the striped material.

As a matter of fact, *she* had preferred the *armoire* against the far wall, but she was not going to tell him that. Instead, she decided to bait him back.

'Did you notice the basket chairs and table on the veranda? Don spotted them at a roadside stall and we stopped, haggled a little—or rather, he did—over the price before we bought them and brought them back here in the Land-Rover. I'm going to make bright cushions for them.'

'I noticed the hand sewing machine,' Jonathan answered casually. 'I'm sure Don will help out by turning the handle for you.'

'I'll do us both a favour and ignore that stupid, insulting remark.'

'By the way,' he went on, 'when it comes to tables, Ceil, you appear to be as obsessed as your great-aunt was.'

'I've already said I'm busy, Jonathan.'

'You haven't told me—what does Don think about your romantic computer?'

'Like me, Don is amazed that more and more people keep sending for questionnaires and, what's more, filling them in and returning them, which just goes to show how hungry people are for someone to love.'

'At a privilege price, of course.'

'Shut up!' Her eyes were blazing with fury now. 'Why should I have to listen to this when I have enough evidence here to show that Computa-mate is a salvation to some people? After all, the whole world is living in a computer age.'

He went on, 'So what you're trying to say is that all over the world computers are changing lives overnight, and what's more, taking a warm, personal interest in clients—that is, without even seeing them?'

'Loneliness, Jonathan, throughout the world, has become the pattern in people's lives. There's a longing for someone special, but they seem powerless to do anything about it—for a number of reasons.'

'Where's the challenge?' he went on. 'Where's the satisfaction in knowing that a computer has been responsible for matching you up?'

'To some, the prospect seems highly attractive.'

'At a hefty fee,' he sneered.

'It happens to be a membership fee, and it's to ensure that clients will continually receive our personal attention.'

'Personal?' He laughed outright. 'Oh, come, Ceil Downing—what do you call personal? You need a man? I've got one—in my computer.'

'People have our phone numbers, Jonathan. We keep in touch—constant touch—by phone or correspondence.'

She rose abruptly from her chair and, in doing so, knocked several folders to the floor. 'Now, look what you've made me do!'

As she stumbled, he caught her. 'You did it to yourself, you little fool.'

Their eyes clung together and, after a long moment, Jonathan took her into his arms and bent his head to kiss her.

Just as her senses were beginning to swim Don Pearson whistled, from somewhere in the house, then he called out, 'Hi? Anyone at home?'

Breaking away from Jonathan, Ceil hissed, 'Don't you ever do that to me again! What is it with you?'

'The same as it is with you, I should imagine.' He pulled her towards him again, and, as he kissed her, he almost crushed the life out of her.

He not only had the power to infuriate her, he had the power to excite her beyond all reasoning, and she found herself clinging to him and, what was more, straining towards him.

What was the next step? she asked herself before she started to drown. Sharing her bed?

Don whistled again, and as she pushed Jonathan away she said, 'You've done nothing but interfere in my life, since the day I met you. Why don't you play the game and leave me alone?'

'Figure that out for yourself,' he told her. 'It shouldn't be too difficult.'

CHAPTER EIGHT

CEIL awoke with a splitting headache. Into the bargain, it was what could possibly be described as a hot, fire-hazard day. She realised that, to get any relief, she would have to take two painkillers, and since she always made a habit of drinking milk after swallowing the tablets she would have to go to the kitchen. She glanced at her bedside clock. Jonathan, she reasoned, would probably still be under the shower.

Seeing him in the kitchen, lean, tanned and athletic-looking and wearing nothing but a pair of sleeping shorts, she froze in the doorway, then turned to leave.

'What's this—the dawn patrol? You don't have to leave on my account.' He turned his dark head to look at her.

They stared at one another for a moment and then his eyes went over the heavy satin robe her mother had given her as a parting gift.

'I thought you'd still be in the shower. It's not a problem. I'll come back later.' Ceil's voice was cool, but she felt strung-up. At a glance, she noticed the strong male beauty of him—the glistening dark hairs on his chest and the hard, flat stomach. As always, there was an almost animal strength about him.

As though the kitchen belonged to him he went on, 'Can I help you?'

'I wanted a glass of milk to take after swallowing two painkillers,' she explained.

'What's the pain in aid of?'

'I have a headache. OK?' Moodily she watched him as he crossed over to the big old-fashioned refrigerator which was still in perfect working condition. Opening the door, he reached inside for the milk. Before leaving Nairobi every afternoon he always bought their bread and milk from a café close to his office.

'You have a headache?' he queried. 'What's the headache in aid of?'

'Don't you get headaches sometimes?' She came right into the kitchen.

He shrugged. 'Sometimes.'

'And what do you do for them?'

'What do you mean, what do I do for them? I wait for them to go, the same way as they come.'

She dismissed this with an irritable gesture. 'Really? However, since you've asked, I'll tell you. You're beginning to pose a problem to me.'

Jonathan glanced up and then banged the refrigerator door.

'I *am*?'

'Yes.'

'Now there's a thing. In what way?' He went over to one of the wall-cabinets and, sliding back a door, took out a glass. 'Say when.' He began to pour.

Ceil was staggered at his arrogance, but, against her will, she found his tanned, well-shaped hands fascinating to watch.

'Half a glass,' she told him.

'I must have missed some of this. What are we talking about? In what way do I pose a problem? Are you referring to the fact that I kissed you and you kissed me back?'

He came over to her and passed her the glass, and as she took it from him his mocking eyes went right over her and the kitchen felt suddenly stifling. She moved away from him.

'You seem to think that I'm yours for the taking!' she snapped. 'I didn't know it was going to be like this, Jonathan!'

'What did you think it was going to be like?' There was a touch of mockery in his tone.

'Well, I didn't think I'd have to ask for breathing-space in my own home. When you work it all out, it doesn't make sense. You do your best to ruffle me up the wrong way. You're mean to Don . . . I shouldn't have to say this, but Don Pearson can come here whenever he likes. That was one of the arrangements. In other words, you go about your affairs and I go about mine. This whole set-up seems to be failing dismally.'

'But I thought we were managing quite well.' She realised he was doing his best to goad her. 'What are we talking about here? Breathing-space? On the whole, you're as wonderfully adept at avoiding me as I am you. If we've slipped up now and then—well, we're only human, after all . . .'

'Speak for yourself!' She took an angry breath. 'Don't work out your sexual frustrations on me. You've always been free to entertain here—you know that. I made that clear from the beginning.'

'In other words,' he said as he looked across at her, 'you were coldly giving me the go-ahead to carry on here with women.'

Feeling at a total disadvantage in her own house, Ceil watched him with moody green eyes as he put the milk back into the refrigerator and slammed the door. She felt a wild spurt of rage. 'I wish you wouldn't slam that door. Jonathan, stop trying to needle me! I'd consider it nothing short of an act of mercy if you stopped turning every situation into some kind of farce.'

'*This* is a farce, let's face it! What's got into you?'

'You know perfectly well what's got into me! I resent the fact that you seem to think you can make a pass at me whenever you're in the mood for some kind of sexual gratification. I don't deserve these insults from you. Try them on someone else.'

'And so you see yourself insulted because I happened to kiss you yesterday?'

'Yes, I do. Stay away from me!'

'But I'm completely mystified. Is that why you kissed me back? Was it to get even? In other words, to insult *me*?'

'Jonathan, I really wanted this to work, you know,' Ceil sighed. 'I really wanted to get on with you.'

'*I* think it's working. It has its moments, of course, but I still think it's working.' Jonathan gave her a taunting half-smile. 'It's quite a lot to ask, after all, sharing a house together and coming to terms with the sexual undercurrents.'

'When it comes to sexual undercurrents, speak for yourself!' she retorted.

He gave her a long look, then laughed. 'Oh, Ceil, you're wholly and unquestionably woman! Let's take this up some other time. It's not convenient right now. I have to get to the office and I'm late enough as it is.'

'Not convenient? Can you tell me when it will be convenient?'

His blue eyes were no longer lazy, but leaping with angry flames.

'Do you know something, Ceil? With you it's always a case of I, I, I and my, my, my. You want to listen to yourself sometimes. I have things to do. Have a nice day—in *your house*!' And he slammed out.

Later, while she was dressing, Ceil heard his car leaving, and soon afterwards the builder and his assistant turned up. The day was under way, she thought.

A wide gallery was now linking the tower to the house. The painter had promised to be back at the end of the month to start painting again, and it suited her to be slotted in with his other customers. Repairs to the pool would be undertaken at a later date.

All was going according to plan—except Jonathan. As she drank her morning tea on the veranda, Ceil gazed at the cover which hid the pool and tried to picture the blue, glittering water which would take its place one day. It seemed reasonable to accept that, if he was still sharing the house, Jonathan would share the pool. She thought of the purple *kikoi* she had bought for him in Mombasa. If you have good legs, she'd quipped, well, show them.

Well, from what she'd seen in the kitchen this morning, Jonathan Caister had a super body—let alone good legs—which was something she'd have to stop thinking about, if she knew what was good for her.

The days continued to flit by. Ceil's office-to-be, at the top of the tower, was now a circle of windows, the panes set into small square frames. Into the bargain, by

designing a domed skylight which went above the level
of the battlements Jonathan had framed the sky.

The desk which Abdel Khaled had supplied had been
set into place after having taken two men half a day to
manoeuvre it up the spiralling iron staircase. At the end
of the day, Ceil had provided beer and snacks for them.
Since she and Jonathan were now on better terms again,
she had also decided that a tower-warming would be in
order.

They were sitting on the veranda before dinner one
evening when she told him of her plans. A jug of chilled
orange juice stood on the table, and as she poured from
it the ice-cubes rattled against the glass.

'A lovely sound,' she laughed. 'Don't you think? It's
been a beast of a day. Well, what do you think about
having a tower-warming?'

Jonathan shrugged. 'It sounds great.'

'Unfortunately the guest list will be very small.' She
laughed again, but she was beginning to feel a little ridiculous now. Who did she think she could ask? Tom and
his wife—Don Pearson... Here the list petered out.

'Who do you intend to invite?' He lifted his glass and
glanced at her over the rim.

'The architect.'

'That goes without saying,' he mocked. 'Who else?'

'Tom and his wife... Don...'

'That's all?' His eyes were still mocking her.

'Jonathan, just you wait until I start meeting people.
I'll give the biggest party—I'll completely outshine my
great-aunt,' she promised.

'That figures. Anything your great-aunt could do you
can do better.'

'That deserves an apology,' she retorted. 'Why do you say these things?'

'Because they're true.'

Ceil was angry and hurt, but she did not show it.

Later in the week, she phoned the ranch and asked to speak to Don, but was told that he had gone into a clinic in Nairobi to have two wisdom teeth extracted.

'Do you know when he'll be back?' Ceil felt betrayed.

'No, not for certain. He was planning to visit his sister for a few days, you see—that is, after the teeth were extracted. Can I get him to ring you when he *does* turn up?'

'No, thank you. I'll be in touch later.' She had been so confident that Don would be at the ranch.

Phoning Tom proved to be another disappointment. He went to some lengths to explain that his wife was far from well and he would not like to leave her.

So that was that. Like an idiot, she thought, she had already started preparing for tomorrow evening. When she had spoken to Jonathan about it he'd said this suited him, but this was not how she'd planned things. She had no desire to be with Jonathan alone at the top of the tower.

As it happened, he phoned her from his office. 'Is the party still on?' he wanted to know.

'Why do you ask? Has something cropped up?'

He laughed. 'No, nothing's cropped up. I just wondered whether you'd like me to buy anything?'

'I've got everything—but I've been a bit of a fool,' said Ceil. 'I was so sure the others could come that I started preparing. Don's gone into a clinic in Nairobi and Miriam Mzima is far from well and Tom doesn't want to leave her. That, I'm afraid, leaves you and me.'

'Why are you afraid?' She heard the mockery in his voice.

'You know what I mean.'

'Go ahead and have the party. You can always arrange another at a later stage. I'm in a party mood, actually,' Jonathan said.

'Are you?'

'Aren't you?'

'I—suppose so. I just thought it might be a bit flat, that's all.'

'Why don't you just take a chance that it won't be?'

After Jonathan had rung off, Ceil sat for a while thinking about what a bungle she'd made of everything. The builders had made it plain that they preferred a party during the lunch-hour, and this was something which she had done for them.

At the end of a busy day, she lost no time in getting into a warm bath, where she lay back and closed her eyes.

The builders had gone and, taking these moments of leisure seriously, she got out of the bath, dried herself and draped the *kanga* which Jonathan had bought for her in Mombasa around her until she was ready to put on the Arab caftan.

She got the shock of her life when she went through to the kitchen to see Jonathan there.

Feeling caught out and vulnerable, with nothing on beneath the *kanga*, she said, 'You're home early. I didn't hear your car arrive, but then I've just got out of the bath. You've caught me at a bad time, actually.'

She saw his blue eyes going right over her. 'When I arrived it was to find you in the bath, apparently, and the french doors wide open to the world,' he remarked.

Ceil thought for a moment. 'I forgot. It's as simple as that.'

'So simple in fact, Ceil, that I passed a very undesirable-looking hobo right near the gates. What is it with you? You're inclined to be too frivolous when it comes to your own safety. You're lethally careless. Why don't you take a few simple precautions when you're here alone? Getting across to you is like trying to get across an obstacle course!'

'I wasn't exactly alone,' she protested. 'Saba was in the garden!'

Jonathan swore under his breath. 'Was he? Are you sure about that?'

'Yes.'

'Quite sure?'

'Quite sure.'

'As it happens, I passed Saba on his bicycle near to the Nairobi turn-off! You were quite alone here. The doors were wide open to every Tom, Dick and Harry, while you were relaxing naked in a bath!'

She was seized by fury. 'Well, that figures. I never bathe fully clad.'

'Don't joke about it, Ceil! Don't you realise how vulnerable you are here? Anybody could come in off the road and—er—rape you, you little fool!'

She caught her breath as he came towards her and tore the *kanga* off her body. Immediately, she saw his intensely blue eyes change as they went over her naked body, and then, tossing the *kanga* over the kitchen stool, he caught her to him with a sudden swift movement. Every nerve in her body seemed to stand on end as she felt his body against her own.

'Thank your lucky stars that it was only me who walked in here to find you like this . . . naked, except for a strip of cloth—beautiful and so desirable that it's just not true.' The message in his eyes was clear as his mouth came down on hers.

Almost immediately she found herself responding to him. After all, she was in love with him—so desperately in love . . .

He took his lips away so that he could cup her breasts in his hands and then kiss them lingeringly. As he kissed her on the mouth again, she responded with a wild, mindless passion.

Suddenly he pushed her away. 'Put some clothes on, for heaven's sake,' he said curtly, before leaving her.

The scene, she realised, had unnerved him, but grabbing the *kanga* from the stool, she shouted, 'Jonathan! You beast!'

Later he knocked on her bedroom door.

'Go away!' Her voice was muffled. 'You're nothing but a beast!'

'Ceil, open the door!'

'No!'

He tried the handle, but found the door locked.

'I want to talk to you!' he shouted.

'I have nothing to say to you. Get out of my house!'

'Don't be difficult. I had no intention of hurting you—you should know that. When I saw you standing there naked, I lost my head . . .'

Suddenly Ceil got up from the side of her bed and went to unlock the door, then she wrenched it open. She was wearing the Arab caftan now.

'When you saw me standing there naked? Who *put* me there naked? I was wearing a *kanga* when I came into the kitchen. *You* tore that *kanga* off me—or have you very conveniently forgotten? How dare you try to blame me?'

'In trying to prove something to you I went too far,' Jonathan admitted. 'The sexual electricity I felt at that moment, Ceil, left no room for reasoning. Everything else just fell away.'

'Yes, I know it did—including my *kanga*! If I *was* vulnerable at any time, Jonathan, I only have you to thank for it. It's only natural that I should have been stretched to the limit when you began to kiss and fondle me. I'm only human. I enjoyed being excited by you. Damn you, Jonathan, you might as well know it—I felt as though I was running into some rather terrible—or terrifying—turbulence—but, thank heavens, I climbed out of it.'

'You climbed out of it?' His eyes held hers. 'The fact is, you were less in control than I was—but at least you're being honest with me.'

'That doesn't give you the right to savage me!' she stormed.

'I had no intention of savaging you, as you put it. OK? The fact still remains that I *did* pass Saba on his bicycle at the turn-off and I *did* see a strange character near your gates. You should be more careful. After all, your aunt had security gates put up in front of all the French doors. Why don't you use them? Even when they're in use, you get all the fresh air and views of the garden you want, without having your home wide open to any intruders who might just decide to pay you an unwelcome visit. Don't you see?'

'Yes, I do, actually. I forgot to close them, that's all. Besides,' her sarcasm was aimed at him, 'I've always felt safe here—until a few minutes ago.'

'You'd feel safe anywhere,' Jonathan retorted angrily. 'That's what worries me.'

'The tower-warming is off! I suppose you know that? I'll just toss everything in the dirt-bin.' Ceil closed the door.

'Ceil, don't be childish.' He pulled the door open before she could lock it.

'Childish?' she retorted. 'So I'm childish? Why is it I seem to be stuck with you? I don't want you in my house.'

'Don't bet on being stuck with me, and don't let this house go to your head. It will still be here long after you've ceased to exist. I'll get out, if that's what you want!'

As she listened to his threat, her heart sank.

CHAPTER NINE

FEELING as tired and depressed as she did, the last thing Ceil felt like doing was climbing the cast-iron staircase to the top of the tower to work. The same old thing, she thought, placing a round glass vase of pink poppies on her desk—arranging romances.

A few moments later she was scanning those questionnaires which had been completed and sent in to Computa-mate. What was she looking for? she asked herself. Hidden meanings? Was there just enough innocence to class what she was doing as above board? Or were some people using this service for something sinister?

Although most of the questionnaires appeared to have been filled in by people genuinely seeking friendship, or something more than friendship, a number of them contained very personal additions.

After a while, Ceil shoved the questionnaires to one side and stood up, then she went to the windows, which followed the curve of the tower, and gazed down at the garden.

This morning she'd heard Jonathan's car as he'd left for his office in Nairobi, and then she had walked round her quiet house. The last thing she wanted was for him to leave—even after what had happened over the *kanga*. She thought about the shock she had seen in his amazing blue eyes when he had discovered she had been wearing nothing beneath the strip of material. Shock had been followed by desire—and what was so frightening was that once the shock, for both of them, had passed, her desire had matched his.

Since food was the last thing on her mind, she did not break for lunch but went on working. Finally she closed down the system at four-thirty.

She was sitting on the long, white-pillared veranda when Jonathan arrived back from work. A tall glass of orange-juice, rattling with melting ice-cubes, stood on the table. The air was warm now, instead of hot, and it was scented by petunias and phlox which had been recently watered by Saba.

'Hello.' Jonathan's voice was curt as he greeted her, then went towards the open french doors which led directly into the lounge. He came back later, after having changed into white cotton trousers and a blue shirt and was carrying a glass of beer, which had a high frothy top to it.

Ceil's hostile green eyes watched him as he sat down at the wicker table. After a moment she said furiously, 'I don't know how you have the nerve to come out here and sit down next to me, as though nothing has happened!'

'What happened was I lost my head and so did you.'

'Isn't that so like you, Jonathan? *So like you!* Sharing this house, as it's supposed to be called, has turned out to be nothing else but an act of intrusion on your part!'

'I told you yesterday, it's no big deal for me to move out,' he said impatiently. 'I'll go tonight, if that's what you want. After all, you did mention on the phone once that you had male company. Maybe you have somebody else lined up to share your house.'

As she listened to him, Ceil began to rack her brains. What was he talking about? What male company? In a flash she remembered. She had been referring to Frank. The cat had been in the house the day she had stormed out of Jonathan's office. He had phoned her, shortly after she had arrived home, and, looking at Frank, who was sharpening his claws on the leg of a rosewood table, she had said, 'I'm in the middle of something—I have company.'

'Complete with its tower,' Jonathan was going on, 'this house has become a sort of medieval castle to you. Something to bring back to life—for what? For you to go on living in for the rest of yours? Like your dear great-aunt before you, it's all you can think of.'

'Why are we fighting about my dear great-aunt, Jonathan?'

'Because, like her, it's a case of my house, my tower, my pool, my garden, my Nandi Flame tree, my gates. No wonder this guy, whoever he was, walked out on her and left her to raise chickens! Like you, she must have sounded like a hot-air balloon. Put it on record, I'm not interested in your bloody house!' He withered her with his angry blue eyes.

'Really?' Ceil was seized by fury now. 'Is that why you suggested moving in?' It was as well, she thought, that he could not see her wounded eyes. She recovered quickly. 'Why were you so keen?'

In one lithe movement he was beside her and, taking her by the shoulders, almost lifted her from the chair.

'Take your hands off me, Jonathan! Don't you turn savage on me!' she stormed.

'I've hardly begun, actually. I've never suffered fools gladly.'

'So you think I'm a fool?'

'Yes, that's exactly what you are. Take a look out there. Go on—take a good look.'

'I know what's out there.' Ceil shook herself free. 'And it doesn't perturb me in the least. I'm not easily intimidated.'

The sun had now set and a few stars were out. Even through the shock and anger she was feeling, she thought she could smell the scents of the nearby game park. In the quickening darkness Jonathan was saying, 'I want you to know one thing. I got by, without your house at the back of things, long before you came on the scene. Do you think I was sitting around wondering what I'd do after I'd sold my house? Don't kid yourself. I suggested moving in here because, after I'd been to see you, I realised no girl should be living here on her own.'

After a moment she said, 'I realise it gets a bit dark out there, but if I'd wanted bright lights I would have come out to Kenya, sold the house and its contents and gone back to England to live in the heart of London. It gets a bit dark here, as I say, but——'

Jonathan laughed shortly. 'It gets a bit dark? You just have to turn to the media to realise what goes on. I'll tell you something, you little fool—right from the word go, you awakened feelings in me I didn't even know I was capable of.'

Ceil's heart missed a beat. 'What kind of feelings?'

He lifted his shoulders. 'Feelings of worry and concern—starting in Mombasa, which, for your information, is essentially a sailor's town. Yet you sailed off to be interviewed by some character and later went off to explore the town at random. Then again, you were quite content to accept my invitation to dinner. And what the hell did you know about me?'

'I took you at face value,' she retorted angrily. 'Besides, you know Tom Mzima.'

'But what does Tom know about me, other than that I'm an architect? You want to ask yourself a few questions before you go leaping into a situation. When I got back from Mombasa, I immediately found myself thinking of you—about what you'd told me—and I decided to look you up, as you know. What I saw here caused me concern. After I left you, I began to worry about you.'

Ceil sat down and looked up at him. 'You know, apart from those silly letters from Tom and your bank manager, I did accept you at face value. After what happened in Mombasa, I forgave you for what you did and I accepted the fact that there'd been a misunderstanding about the disco. The next day, I felt safe exploring the old town with you. Quite honestly, I wasn't all that happy shopping on my own in Mombasa. I've travelled a bit on the Continent and I'm aware of muggings and bag-snatching, believe it or not. I was prepared to be hassled—but nothing ventured, nothing gained, after all.'

'And that just about sums you up in a nutshell, Ceil. Don't you see?' Jonathan sat down. 'Nothing ventured, nothing gained appears to be your motto.'

When she did not answer he said, very softly, 'Ceil?'

She laughed a little, then sobered. 'If I *did* have any fears before you came they were totally groundless. I now have fears of a different sort.'

'What sort of fears?'

'Fears, Jonathan, of falling into a pattern where casual lovemaking is introduced into my life and then taken completely for granted. I'm feeling incredible tension. It would be so easy to let you make love to me because I-I-I'm-ripe for it.' She could hardly tell him that she was in love with him. 'If this—sharing a house together—is going to work, stop putting me in a position where I'm tempted beyond all reason to enjoy what would amount to nothing but sexual freedom.'

With measured brutality he said, 'Are you saving yourself for some special guy? In England, maybe? Or even out here? Someone you don't get to see all that often?'

'Why do you want to know? What difference does it make to you?' Her breathing was suddenly difficult. Was Jonathan in love with her?

'Now that's a stupid answer, isn't it? Naturally it makes a difference, for the simple reason that I'd begin to ask myself what the hell I'm doing here, worrying about some stupid female.'

His answer was like a chill wind. 'I see. Well, like you, I *did* have something going but, to quote you, "whatever it was" is over. To get back to sharing the house, though. We might as well be open about this—I do want you to stay on. I really do. I mean,' Ceil lifted her shoulders, 'I've had to adjust to a complete new lifestyle out here. It's all strange to me. I've enjoyed—up to a point, that is—having you here.'

'So I do provide a service? That, I take it, of helping you to adjust to your new lifestyle?' Jonathan's voice had a hard edge to it. 'Look, we'll take it from there. I guess I can handle the sexual electricity—and so can you.'

After a while they smoothed things over and it was time to think about the evening meal—an asparagus tart and salads—which Ceil had prepared earlier. As they sat down to eat on the veranda, there was the rumble of distant thunder.

Conversation between them had thawed sufficiently to focus on wild-life, and even drifted to the late Miss Ceil Downing.

'Tom hinted at an unhappy—from what I gather— love-affair—when she was young, of course,' Ceil remarked.

'Let's hope the same thing doesn't happen to you, in that case.'

There was an apprehensive silence.

'Why should it happen to me?' she asked, in a tight voice. 'I can't see the connection. We're not talking about me, we're talking about her...'

'As usual.' His voice had a warning edge of anger now. 'As usual, Ceil, huh?'

'I don't think so.'

'Anyway, what were you going to say?' asked Jonathan.

'I was going to say that I don't intend ending up having a romantically reckless romance.' She reached for her glass. Why did it always end like this? she asked herself.

'And so you do think she was reckless—that is, after he walked out on her?'

'Jonathan, you can be so cruel! He didn't just walk out on her.'

'How do you know?' he snapped. 'Maybe he got sick of asking her to give up this house and marry him. In other words, maybe this house got in the way!'

There was a sudden clap of thunder which followed a particularly vivid flash of lightning, and a moment later Saba hurried out to clear the table.

The storm broke, and it was going to be a storm second to none, Ceil thought as she hurried indoors, but with Jonathan in the house it would not be so terrifying.

CHAPTER TEN

IT WAS a clear, sunny day after the storm which had raged
the night before. Getting up from her desk, Ceil went
to stand at the windows that encircled the top of the
tower. It had taken time getting used to working up here
alone in the mystical silence.

Down below, in the garden, Frank seemed a little too
interested in the bird life which was going on around
him. Two courting doves had flown down from a tree
and were strutting about the lawn. Crouching low now,
the Siamese cat had begun to stalk them.

From her high viewpoint Ceil yelled, '*Frank!* Just you
leave those birds alone, you devil!'

At that moment the birds took off, leaving a furious
blue-eyed Frank with a lashing tail, and Ceil found
herself laughing at his rage. 'Good,' she called. 'Good!'

With some reluctance she went back to her desk, but,
after only a few minutes, got up again and went back
to the windows. Somehow she could not concentrate.
She didn't feel like working at the computer and she certainly didn't feel like typing the usual letters which ac-
companied the questionnaires.

Looking down at the garden again, she saw Frank
watching a blue-headed lizard which was sunning itself
on the lower branch of a wild tree.

'Oh, no!' she moaned in despair. 'What's the matter
with that cat today?'

127

As she clattered down the spiral staircase, she found herself praying that she wouldn't be too late.

It took a few moments to unlock the heavy iron-studded door in a central archway which was hardly ever used now that the tower was linked to the house.

'I'm going to break this up once and for all,' she shouted at Frank. 'You horrible little beast! Come here; you're going into the kitchen, and then maybe I'll get some work done!'

Lifting the squirming cat into her arms, she went back into the tower and through the arch that led to the gallery.

'Stop it! Frank, you're scratching me!'

Once in the kitchen, she closed the door and then looked out some chopped chicken livers and a bowl of milk, while Frank miaowed loudly and rubbed himself against her legs. Making sure that he couldn't get up to mischief again, Ceil closed the windows and the door which led to the patio, for although the wrought-iron security gate was in place Frank was slim and wiry enough to get through the ornamental scrollwork. Closing the other door, she made her way back to the tower.

The area was cool, with a small fountain, and she had been lucky enough to buy several pink orchids which were in bloom, and as a result she was soon side-tracked into admiring them before going towards the iron stairs.

Her sitting-room was on the second level and, as usual, she gave it an admiring glance. The divan which her great-aunt had slept on during the Mau Mau rebellion had now been moved down to this level. She'd had the upholsterers make a frilled peacock-blue cover and the divan was piled high with cushions in vibrant colours of blue, purple, rose and gold. By also using a small wicker table and two wicker chairs, she had created an inviting sitting-room for herself—not that she ever used it.

Since the scene of the *kanga*, as she had come to think of it, she and Jonathan had reached a better understanding, after having talked about it the following day.

He had taken her to see the house he had now bought in Karen. Like a number of other attractive houses in the vicinity, this house had been around a long time and needed attention, but it had charm. What was so strange was that Ceil could visualise her own furniture in it.

As she settled herself behind her desk again and struggled to work she felt restless. Her moody eyes strayed to the circular stone walls of the tower. She had bought a large map of Kenya and kept a record of computer successes by using pins with brightly coloured bead heads. The map formed a feature, as did a number of coloured prints which had been sent in by happy couples. Several people had even sent her crimson hearts, which had also found their way to the walls.

Always there were flowers—either from the garden, which Saba was slowly bringing under control, or from her favourite flower-seller in Nairobi. It was a romantic-looking environment in which to work, but nobody ever saw it. Everything was done by computer, correspondence and telephone.

With a sigh she began typing.

Dear Ms Darua,
Welcome, and thank you for your enquiry regarding Computa-mate. We have pleasure in explaining the procedure to you.

Suddenly she stiffened and broke off typing to listen to the footsteps of someone using the spiralling iron staircase.

'Oh, God,' she whispered, 'please help me. Please! I've forgotten to lock the heavy door to the tower!'

Stark fear paralysed her, so that she just sat there rigidly. She had been so side-tracked by Frank and pink orchids that she had completely forgotten it. As her shocked eyes met and held the dark eyes of a man she had never seen before, the first thing she thought of was rape, and her sun-warmed tower was suddenly cold and full of menace.

Keep calm, she told herself. Don't panic.

He was saying, with cool arrogance, 'I passed a man on a bicycle just past your gates. He explained that he works for you and told me where you'd be working.'

Ceil felt fear immobilise her and then, gathering her wits together, she said, 'I don't believe we have an appointment, Mr...?'

This man only had to force her down to the level below, she was thinking wildly, where he would already have seen the inviting pillow-laden divan. She tried desperately not to show that she was shaking.

'Yarda Lazar. The name should ring a bell.'

'It doesn't,' she said. 'Should it?'

'Allow me to refresh your memory, Miss Downing— or why don't you refer to that white box? It's supposed to possess supernatural powers, I believe. In my case, however, there appears to have been—what would they call it—syntax error? Anyway, it succeeded in wrecking my life. In other words, I ended up marrying the wrong dame.'

'How do you know my name, since it doesn't appear on our letterhead?' she asked.

'Yeah, I was coming to that, actually. That was a crafty move on your part, wasn't it? But let's just say I found out, through a little research in the right direction, and leave it at that. You've got to be in the know, as they say.'

Without waiting to be invited, he sat down on the chair opposite her. Apart from Jonathan, Don Pearson and Tom Mzima, this man was her first visitor—and an unwelcome one at that.

'Mr Lazar, I shouldn't have to point this out to you, but we *do* have a clause in our questionnaire which reads—and I quote— "All information is accepted in good faith and we cannot be held responsible for incorrect information given". You must have read that clause, surely?'

'And you think that clause covers you?' There was hostility in his voice. 'Let me tell you something, Ceil Grace Downing. *I* have, as I said, been doing a little research of my own, without the help of a computer, I might add, and I've made quite a few discoveries—one being that your Abdel Khaled in Mombasa is quietly running a sex racket on the sidelines. In other words, he's been responsible for the downfall of innocent girls who've ended up, often unwillingly, as the playthings of wealthy men!'

'That's simply not true!' she exclaimed. 'How dare you come here and make such accusations? You just have to take a look at those photos and hearts on the wall. Do they look like the gestures of unwilling playthings

of wealthy men? They were sent voluntarily, by de-
lighted members.'

'Spare me the sales talk,' he snapped.

Ceil wished she could stop shaking. 'I suggest, Mr
Lazar, that you take your grievances to Mr Khaled in
Mombasa. And now, I have an appointment in Nairobi.
My fiancé will be here at any minute to pick me up.'

She saw him blink. 'Since you're going out, I suggest
we have lunch together one day. I'll be in touch. Before
I take Abdel Khaled to the cleaners, I want to put you
wise.'

'Are you threatening me by any chance?' she asked.

'No, not at all. And by the way, you'll be quite safe
with me. I don't attack women. You owe it to me, and
to yourself, for that matter, to listen to what I have to
say. After that, I suggest you get yourself another job.'

After he had gone, Ceil's thoughts were a network of
anxiety. She lost no time in locking the iron-hinged and
studded door to the tower, then she let a yowling Frank
out of the kitchen.

Pride, of course, would keep her from telling Jonathan
about this. After all, he'd done nothing but criticise her
work. He had also gone out of his way to show her that
she should be more security-minded when she was here
on her own—and what had she done? She'd left the door
wide open to any Tom, Dick and Harry who might be
passing her gate while she sat up in her sky-framed tower
with the coloured prints and red hearts all about her,
and not even a dog to bark a warning. Jonathan would
be the very last person she would confide in. Even Tom
Mzima had warned her, from the beginning.

Yarda Lazar phoned a week later, just when she had begun to think he'd forgotten all about her.

'I'll pick you up for lunch,' he told her.

A feeling of blind rage overtook Ceil. 'How dare you pester me again? I'm warning you—leave me alone!'

'Whether you like it or not, you're going to hear all about the marriage that turned into a circus. You owe that to me. You're also going to hear a lot more,' he added.

'I owe you nothing! Get off my line!'

He went on as if nothing had happened, 'We'll go to that nice place on Langata Road—the Carnivore. They have an excellent selection of venison—or you might prefer lamb, or skewered chicken—it's up to you. All you have to do, my dear Ceil, is eat and listen. Let's make it tomorrow, since I've caught you on the hop. Tomorrow—and, once again, I don't attack women.'

'I'm going out with my fiancé tomorrow.' This was, in one respect, true, since Jonathan had suggested a day off from work for both of them, and they were going to the African Adventure snake and crocodile park.

'Break it, Ceil.' His voice was dangerously quiet.

'I can't.' She felt, quite suddenly, that she had lost control of her life.

'Doesn't this guy work for a living?' He laughed. 'Anyway, where are you going?'

'I see no reason to tell you. Let's just say that he's reserved a table for lunch.'

'I said—where?' This time his voice had a nasty tone to it. 'I'm a stickler for the truth, by the way.'

'We're going to—a crocodile park.'

'I see. Well, you go to your crocodile park and we'll make it soon after. Have a nice day.'

She wondered whether she should, after all, confide in Jonathan—or Tom. On an impulse, she dialled Tom's number and was told that Tom had gone to Lamu for two weeks, since his wife had been ordered by her doctor to take a vacation. In desperation, Ceil phoned the game ranch. Don might just be back—but he wasn't.

A moment later she rang Jonathan. 'I'd like to ask your advice about something, Jonathan,' she began.

He laughed softly. 'That's not like you, to ask for my advice. Are things getting out of hand?'

Her heart took a leap. 'What do you mean?'

'I mean, are some of the blind dates you arrange with such total abandon giving you trouble?'

'Oh, I can't talk to you——' she began, but he broke in.

'What's worrying you, Ceil?'

In the circumstances, she thought it best to lie. 'I just wondered whether you knew where I could buy a second-hand fax machine.'

'What do you want a fax machine for, for heaven's sake?' He sounded impatient.

'To connect me to Mombasa.'

'Oh, come, Ceil! Where's all this going to end?'

She drew a long breath. 'Actually, Jonathan, I've just changed my mind,' she said.

Replacing the receiver, she thought, I'll just have to manage Yarda Lazar my way. I have no option.

When the phone rang again, she ignored it.

CHAPTER ELEVEN

ON THE drive to the African Adventure snake and crocodile park, thoughts of Yarda Lazar kept distracting Ceil until she felt brittle enough to snap.

At one stage, Jonathan turned to look at her with impatient blue eyes. 'How about helping out with a little conversation? Are you still brooding about that fax machine?'

'I've forgotten all about the fax machine, as it happens. I've been listening to *you* talk,' she answered.

'Really? I don't think you've heard one word.'

'You were talking about your work—about the escalating costs of clay bricks, timber and labour, which could mean the end of the traditional house in this country.'

'So you find the housing problems of Kenya interesting?' The cynical amusement in his voice infuriated her. 'But, on the other hand, you're regretting taking a day off from your warm-hearted computer, is that it?'

'For once, Jonathan, leave the computer out of this. Everything with you revolves around that computer— and the house, of course.'

'No, that's where you're wrong. Everything with *you* revolves around the house.'

'Why are you being so vile to me?' she flamed.

'Use your imagination.' Jonathan turned to look at her. 'Men are usually vile to women they're in love with.'

Although she felt her nerves tighten Ceil said, 'You're not in love with me, even if you do happen to go on as if you have some claim on me.'

'I do have a claim on you, and you know it.' His voice was soft. 'You know and I know that the claim I have on you is that you want me as much as I want you. When that time comes—which could even be tonight— I don't want to be reminded that I take second place to a house called Mnarani. I guess I could live with the computer, but when it comes to another man or a house—no way. Anyway, what's on your mind, Ceil?'

'Nothing's on my mind.'

'You'd better start thinking about your own ro- mance—which is starting in earnest, as from today.'

'Ending where, Jonathan? Like the romance you had going with Xenia—washed up? You know—"whatever it was, it's over"? Tell me, as a matter of interest, is that why my house plays such an important role? Be- cause, when "whatever it was" is over and it's time for you to move on you'll always have the house as an excuse? The house got in the way, you'll say. I couldn't live with it...'

After he had parked the car, they got out and walked towards the gates to the park and Jonathan bought tickets from an attendant who sat at the window of a log cabin.

In a split-pole fenced area a display of dancing was going on to the hammering of drums and shrill whistles, and most of the visitors had gathered there to watch.

The park was laid out on a rise which, since it happened to be an unusually chilly day, seemed to be catching a sneaky breeze. In some areas it was actually cold beneath the shade of the many jacaranda and blue-gum trees.

On a level above the crocodile enclosure, the glass-fronted habitats of the snakes were completely under shade and, to Ceil, the snakes looked cold and lonely. As she and Jonathan passed from window to window the reptiles—sometimes one to a dwelling—were mostly sleeping but, exhibiting its sheer hatred at being a prisoner, an Egyptian spitting cobra reared its hooded head and spat at them.

For a second Ceil forgot that glass divided them, and she stepped back in fright, right into Jonathan's arms. Laughing softly, he tightened his arms about her, then turned her round to face him. His dark blue eyes went to her lips and she watched him as he bent his head to kiss her.

'Don't push your luck, Jonathan!' She pushed him away and began to walk on. Over her shoulder she said, 'I thought snakes were supposed to like sun, and yet here they are in heavy shade. I think it's disgusting! Can you imagine what it must be like here in winter?'

'The sun changes position in the winter, or didn't they teach you that at school?' he mocked.

Wanting to quarrel with him, she said, 'The snakes, especially those on their own, all look so lonely.'

'Snakes are normally shy and secretive, anyway,' he told her, and she could see he was becoming impatient. He turned to look at her. 'And stop acting like that spitting cobra back there. Like him, when you find yourself cornered you spit out your venom, aiming, if possible, at the face of your presumed enemy. Since when have you and I become such enemies, Ceil? Since you made the unsettling discovery that you're in love with me?'

She began to walk on, and after a moment, he followed her. 'What are we fighting for? Do you know?' he persisted.

When she made no reply he mocked, 'In case you don't know—in mythology, the dragon has been depicted as a ravishingly beautiful girl with long, flowing hair. Its fire-breathing properties have been referred to as a burning thirst or hunger. It's a will which desires, yet has nothing capable of satisfying it, except its own self.'

'Is that supposed to be getting at me?' Her green eyes were accusing.

As they walked on Jonathan said, 'Don't let's fight—especially as I'm going to make love to you tonight. We're going to satisfy that hunger.'

'We aren't, you know. What makes you think I'll want to?'

'You'll want to, by the time I've finished with you.'

'You're very sure of yourself, but if I say I don't want to—believe me, we won't.'

'I've had some experience when it comes to making women do things they don't want to do.' He took her hand and, turning it over, kissed her palm.

In love with him as she was, she felt her mood begin to improve as they strolled about, and especially when they were joined by a Staffordshire bull terrier, who obviously belonged to the ranger and his wife, living nearby.

Ceil doubled over with laughter as the dog succeeded in rocking the low pedestal which was used to display the toothy skull of a crocodile and then sprang back and stared at the teeth, which now posed a threat to him.

Later they joined a number of noisy schoolchildren in a small building used for showing films and which smelled strongly of tar. A film was in progress, and the activities of Nile crocodiles and monitor lizards only half held the attention of the pushing and shoving children, who hissed at every opportunity.

'This is fun,' Ceil said, forgetting all about Yarda Lazar.

After the film Jonathan said, 'Well, did you learn anything about Nile crocodiles and monitor lizards?'

She laughed. 'Nothing, except that they grow to six feet or more in length.'

They were still sitting in the theatre, which was just a tar-smelling space with a screen at one end and a tiny projection-room at the other. Jonathan's eyes went to her lips. 'You know something? I happen to care for you very much. What you do, what happens to you, means everything to me. I mean it when I say I love you.'

After a moment she said, 'I might as well admit it, Jonathan—I'm in love with you too. I don't always *like* you, but I do love you.'

He stood up and reached for her hand. 'To be continued,' he said softly, 'when we get back.'

Where was this going to end? she asked herself. And when? Tonight? In bed? Her senses began to swim.

The exterior of the small restaurant was like an old-fashioned house. It was painted fir-green, and the woodwork was white—white casements, white veranda pillars and wicker chairs and tables, with pink and blue cloths and cushions, were set at intervals on the wooden veranda floor.

Jonathan opened one half of the french doors leading to the restaurant then stood back for Ceil to enter.

Her eyes scanned the area for a table for two and she noticed the dried flowers, which looked lovely.

Although she had told Yarda Lazar that her fiancé had reserved a table at a crocodile park, this was not really true. It was a case of finding a suitable table or waiting until one became vacant.

As it happened, the restaurant was practically full, and, turning to Jonathan, she said, 'It will have to be right over there in the corner. Everybody seems to have made straight for here, after the dancing.'

As she made for the table, she stiffened as she found herself looking into the dark eyes of the very man she had just been thinking of a short while ago, and she realised that she had no option but to keep moving, but something went cold in her. What was this man up to? And how stupid could she get? How many crocodile safari parks had she supposed were scattered around Nairobi? What a fool she had been to practically tell him where they were lunching.

A few moments later, Yarda Lazar came over to their table and was saying, 'So, Ceil, how's it going? As usual, you're looking very glamorous. How's work in the old look-out tower? Any more photos added to your famous collection? Any more big red cardboard hearts?'

Deciding to play it cool, she said, 'What are *you* doing here?' Her green eyes had a furious message for him and she made no move to introduce him to Jonathan.

'You triggered my mind off when you mentioned the other day that you were going to be having lunch here. I thought—gee, you know, I've never been there. I must say, though, I had no idea it was today.'

At that moment their food conveniently arrived and Yarda Lazar glanced at his watch. 'Well, I guess it's back to the old salt-mines. I'll be seeing you, Ceil. In any case, we have a date for lunch at the Carnivore.' He turned to look down at Jonathan. 'Sorry, I didn't catch your name?'

'It's something you can brood about on your way back to the salt-mines,' Jonathan answered.

Yarda laughed at that and then, having the nerve to ruffle Ceil's ash-blonde hair, he said, 'You want to brush up your manners.'

Moodily Ceil watched him as he went towards the french doors.

Jonathan had lifted his knife and fork. 'Well, well! So you've been having a visitor to the faded pink fortress and I didn't even know.' He spoke with acid sarcasm.

'He came on business—and stop referring to my house as the faded pink fortress. I don't like it.' Her voice was as brittle as she felt.

'Business, huh? I was always given to understand that the situation of entertaining visitors in your office was not something likely to arise. I mean,' he lifted his shoulders, 'you said yourself, no visitors. Of course, you do have that charming little sitting-room on the next level, with the divan piled high with pillows.'

'Maybe I do make the odd exception,' she retorted angrily, 'to have someone to my office. After all, you don't know everything that goes on in my life.'

'Apparently I don't. You know...' he dropped rather than put down his knife and fork and sat back and looked at her '...when the girl who's just said "I love you" is a cheat, no more fertile ground for conflict could exist.'

'I'm entitled to visitors, Jonathan!' She wanted to hit back at him. 'Besides, I didn't *exactly* say I love you— I said I don't always like you——'

'I know what you said!' His eyes were blazing. 'I know what you said.'

'I don't want to have to explain about Yarda Lazar.' She said his name without thinking. 'He—he's just a friend.'

'How did you meet him, and when? Under the circumstances, I'd be interested to know, actually.'

When she made no attempt to answer him he said, 'Ceil? I asked you a question. Why don't you answer?'

'Because you won't want to know how and when I met him. The point is, I met him.'

'The point is, I hope you know what you're doing?'

'I always know what I'm doing. I consider myself to be capable and competent when it comes to running my own life. He's just someone I know.' Theatrically, Ceil raised her glass. 'I mean, *you* know people...Xenia, for instance.'

'Do you know what he reminds me of?'

'I'm not interested in what he reminds you of!'

'In any case, I'll tell you. He reminds me of a vulture waiting in a tree.'

'Well, Jonathan, he'll have a damn long wait, that's all I can say.'

'In that case, drop him!' He was really angry now.

'What am I supposed to say? Yes, Jonathan, I'll do just that? Oh, come on!'

'You're the best judge of whether you should say that. Apparently, though, I don't understand you one bit.'

'Jonathan, let me explain——'

'You don't have to explain, Ceil. It all falls into pattern.'

'Oh, does it?' She was furious now. 'My advice to you, Mr Caister, is not to judge me on your imagination. OK?'

By the time they got back to Mnarani they were barely speaking, and that night, Ceil went to bed feeling utterly drained and depressed.

How could she confide in a man like Jonathan?

CHAPTER TWELVE

YARDA LAZAR phoned a week later, and Ceil took a calming breath as she listened to him. How much more was she to take from this man? she asked herself.

Into the bargain, Siamese Frank had been missing for three days, and she was frantic with worry. Every day, after a cold and remote Jonathan had left for his office, she had virtually combed the garden and nearby area in her search for the cat. She'd driven along the dirt road, looking for him, and hopelessly scanned the roadside.

'What exactly is it you want of me, Mr Lazar?' she asked angrily. 'I don't need this aggravation.'

'I'm about to blow the lid off Computa-mate,' he told her, 'and you should know the reasons why. I'll pick you up for lunch at the Carnivore. Look, you can check me out. Phone the Mañana Hotel. That's where I worked as manager before I was fired—as a direct result of being married to a floozie.'

'I'll meet you at the Carnivore,' Ceil found herself saying.

Before leaving home, she took the precaution of phoning the Mañana Hotel, and what Reception had to say about Yarda Lazar confirmed what he had told her. Mr Lazar had had domestic problems and his dismissal had nothing to do with his work, or his reputation.

As she drove towards Nairobi, Ceil's anxious eyes scanned the roadside for Frank. Had he landed up in

the Nairobi national game park? Her heart fainted at
the thought of twenty-five-foot-long pythons and wild
dogs which hunted in packs. Still hurt and furious with
Jonathan, she had kept the worry of Frank to herself.

It did not take her long to reach the conclusion that
Yarda Lazar was moody, intense and unpredictable. At
the moment he was talking about his wife. 'She was a
turn-on but, boy, did I have a lot to learn! At first, I
was blinded. I thought, this is it. This is great! What
happened, though? I'll tell you. We were anything but
compatible. So what went wrong with the computer?
Was it a case of virus?' He laughed unpleasantly.

'Why keep blaming the computer?'

'What about user ignorance?' His black eyes blazed.

Eventually they parted next to where her car was
parked. 'I'll be in touch. I have lots more to tell you,'
he said.

'If you have any more complaints, Mr Lazar, I suggest
you contact Mombasa,' she told him. 'What you've told
me over lunch today concerns Mr Khaled, not me. I certainly am not aware of being involved in any shady
dealings.'

There was still no sign of Frank when she got home
and her depression, frustration and anger were
overwhelming.

During what was left of the afternoon she tried to
interest herself in rearranging books on the shelves, next
to the fireplace in the lounge.

Suddenly she stiffened as she heard Jonathan arriving, and, before she could do anything about es-
caping to her room, he came through to the kitchen.
Although she now had herself under control, she kept

her back to him as she reached into a wall cabinet for plates.

'Hi.' His voice was elaborately polite. 'If I don't have a glass of orange juice I'll keel over. It's as hot as hell outside!' When she made no reply he went on, 'Why isn't Frank eating? When I come through to the kitchen in the morning, his food is untouched.'

Ceil swung round. 'Is that all you have to say? Why isn't Frank eating? His food is untouched!' Her voice was accusing and bitter. 'Not once, Jonathan, have you bothered to ask about him.'

'I've just asked after him,' he snapped.

'Well, I'll tell you. Frank's been gone for days. I'm frantic with worry.' Her voice broke. 'Where can he be-e...? He's probably found himself in the game park. For all I know, he might have been eaten by a hyena—or a lion. He could have been crushed alive by a python!'

'Why attack me like this, Ceil?' Jonathan exploded. 'Why didn't you tell me? Be reasonable!'

'You're the one who's not being reasonable! I just can't talk to you any more. There've been things I've been wanting to ask you...wanting to tell you...'

He came over to her and, lifting her hand, began to stroke her wrist with his fingers. When she weakened and began to cry, he took her into his arms.

'Cats do this,' he told her. 'They go on the razzle.' When she made no reply he said softly, 'Ceil? Come on...' He lifted her hair and kissed the nape of her neck. 'I'll go on a search.'

'I've searched until I'm blue in the face!' she sobbed. 'Everything seems to be going wrong lately,' she sniffed. 'I wish I could get away for a few days.'

After a short silence he said, 'How would you like to go away early next week? That is, if I can arrange it. I've been invited to join a safari, and although I turned the invitation down maybe the offer still stands. It's a private safari.'

'Oh, I couldn't go,' she protested. 'Frank might turn up.'

'Leave food and instructions for Saba to feed him.'

'In any case, how do you know I'd be welcome?'

'It's an open invitation.'

'I see. In other words, it was expected you'd want to take Xenia, wasn't it?'

'Not necessarily.' He shrugged.

Ceil found she was tempted. It would be marvellous to get away for a few days, before the builders returned to begin on further alterations. It would get her away from Yarda Lazar.

'I can almost read your mind, Ceil,' said Jonathan. 'Forget about the computer—you're even beginning to resemble it!—or would you like to take it on safari with you? I might be able to get a battery for it. Who knows?'

'As it happens, I'm not thinking of the computer. You always bring that up.'

'Just as you keep bringing Xenia up. Xenia means nothing to me now—just a good friend. But what are you worried about—your house, as usual? Or that I'll try to make love to you?'

'Yes, that is exactly what I'm worrying about—and, what's more, that I'll end up letting you.'

He laughed sarcastically. 'I'll try to make love to you, of course, and not expect *too* much. But why not let nature take its course?'

'Because nature has a strange way of creating havoc. Look at earthquakes, for instance. I don't want an earthquake in my life.'

'Even if there's an earthquake, you're one person who will survive. You and your house.'

'Am I?' Her voice contained anger now. 'You don't plan an earthquake, Jonathan. Anyway, I'll have to think about the safari. When do you have to know my answer?' she asked.

He thought for a moment. 'I'll have to contact Evan— to find out if the invitation is still open. Evan's the guy who runs these safaris. There was a last-minute cancellation and he asked if I'd care to make up the party. The others are Americans. For all I know he might have asked somebody else.' He glanced at his watch. 'I suppose I could phone him now.' He lifted his lashes and gave her a searching look. 'If the offer is still open, what's it to be?'

Although Ceil recognised the desire she felt for him to make love to her she said, 'I'd like to go.'

'In that case, I'll give him a ring.'

'When he came back he said, 'He says he'll be more than pleased to have us.'

As she spent the following day shopping for safari clothes, Ceil almost forgot her worries.

The safari left Nairobi for a one-night stop-over at a ranch owned by a third-generation Kenyan and his blonde Scandinavian wife, and it came as a surprise to Ceil when she discovered that it was the same ranch she had visited with Jonathan, for dinner, and then again with Don Pearson.

'Why didn't you tell me the stop-over was to be at the ranch where Don works?' she asked.

'Because you didn't ask,' Jonathan mocked.

Don's face, when he saw Ceil with Jonathan, was like a mask, but the disappointed expression in his eyes betrayed him, and since she had at no time encouraged him, Ceil felt irritated.

At the crack of dawn the following morning, they were on their way, heading for the Amboseli, under Kilimanjaro, crossing bush-covered country which was sprinkled with flat-topped thorn trees. There was game to be seen and, occasionally, a Masai homestead, enclosed by a thorn fence.

Before taking the turn to the game park, they were taken to see sellers of curios, and Ceil had her first glimpse of warriors of the Masai.

Spurting up dust and small stones, the safari trucks were on their way again, rattling along a corrugated dirt road. From time to time the drivers slackened speed to allow their excited passengers to view game.

Lake Amboseli came as a shock, for it was just a salt pan.

'Is it always like this?' Ceil turned to look at a devastatingly handsome and khaki-clad Jonathan, as they took the main track round the edge of the lake.

'Except for an occasional pool of water in the rainy season, yes.' He laughed a little. 'Are you disappointed?'

'Well, yes.' She also laughed. 'I must admit I didn't expect to see an empty pan of saline dust. I expected to see a huge expanse of shimmering water.'

'Will a phantom lake do?' His expression was mocking.

'A phantom lake?' She was puzzled.

'We'll probably see one before long. It's quite a spectacular mirage.'

'Oh, I hope we do, Jonathan!' She was in love with him and she was beginning to enjoy herself, and she realised that she would not like to have missed this wonderful experience with him.

Near to camp, the safari truck in front—occupied by Evan, his wife Bette and an American couple, developed a flat tyre, and while the wheel was being changed several Masai tribesmen, their hair covered with red ochre, seemed to appear from nowhere and stood around, leaning on their spears and gazing at the activity around them. They were tall and fine-featured and clad in toga-like garments, and Ceil was fascinated by their large bead earrings and leg and arm bands.

Eventually the wheel was changed and the convoy was able to continue. There was a strange beauty about the swampy and misty Amboseli, and Ceil felt her nerves tighten up. Her first taste of being on safari, she thought, as she noticed the tented camp.

The camp was on the Tanzanian border at the foot—almost—of the snow-capped Kilimanjaro, and it was situated in a clearing of acacia trees. Because of the mist, however, they could not see the mountain, but in any case Ceil was too busy coping with the jolting discovery, a few minutes later, that she was to share a dark green sleeping tent with Jonathan, to notice anything.

'Kilimanjaro, in case you've been wondering,' Jonathan was saying very nonchalantly, 'can only usually be seen at dawn and dusk, when the mists lift.'

'I see.' Her voice was cool and a little sarcastic. 'I *was* wondering. Thanks for telling me.'

'This is it, then. I hope you'll be comfortable.' His blue eyes met and held hers, before they entered the tent.

Inside there were two canvas washstands, a table with a mirror, soap, lotions, tubes of sun-block, towels, face-cloths, two high iron beds with impeccable sheets, pillow-cases and blankets. A lantern stood on a second table and there were two chairs. A can of insect spray had also been provided, along with a flashlight.

'I'll show you how to work the shower,' Jonathan was saying. He led the way to the reed shower stall, which had a board to stand on. 'You lower the bucket from the tree, like this. Fill it with hot water—which will be brought to you, by the way—then hoist the bucket up again.' He turned to smile at her wooden face. 'Simple, but it works.'

Going back into the tent, he went on casually—a bit too casually, Ceil thought, 'Which bed do you want?'

'That one.' Her voice was strained. After a moment he came over to her and put his hands on her shoulders.

'Look, I want you to relax with me,' he said gently.

He looked strong and self-confident and his body heat seemed to spread to her, and she wondered how she could relax—now.

'Don't I look relaxed?'

'No.' He smiled faintly.

'You didn't tell me...' she began.

'And, being your usual reckless self, you didn't ask, right?'

Ignoring this remark, she went on, 'I've never been on a safari before. Actually, I thought we'd be going to a lodge or staying in *bandas*, or something—like last night.' She lifted her shoulders and let them drop. 'I don't know. I just don't *know* what I expected.'

'Does it make any difference?' Jonathan queried.

Her laugh was brittle. 'Well, of course it makes a difference!'

'Unfortunately, Ceil, I have no magic solution to offer.'

'And *I* can't just walk away, can I? So I'll just have to make the best of it. Since we already happen to be sharing a house, that should make things a lot easier for both of us.'

'These people conduct luxury safaris, in every sense of the word, and the advantages are endless—but having your own bedroom, Ceil, doesn't come into it.'

In a tight voice she said, 'I appreciate that. As you pointed out a moment ago, being my usual reckless self, I didn't ask.'

'As far as tourists are concerned, they believe they're roughing it, complete with gas-powered refrigerator and freezer, and that gives them tremendous satisfaction.' He was smiling, but his eyes were serious, as he went on looking at her. Obviously he was trying to put her at ease, she thought.

'*I* feel *I'm* roughing it—but being terribly pampered while doing so. I'm not complaining. I feel privileged to have been invited. Thank you.'

As they went outside, Ceil decided to make the best of it, and glanced around at the set-up. There were other tents of heavy canvas, and small tables and chairs were placed around what would be the camp-fire at night.

Jonathan pointed out the dining—or mess—tent.

'I can smell bread baking,' Ceil said. 'It smells wonderful.'

He took her arm. 'Come, I'll show you how it's baked.'

The bread in question was being baked in a large metal box which was half buried in the ground and smothered in burning coals. Glancing at the cooks, in their white safari suits and striped butchers' aprons, Ceil said, 'They didn't waste much time in getting started, did they?'

'The advantages of a luxury safari, Ceil, are endless, as I remarked a moment ago. The camp had been prepared for us. All we had to do was arrive.'

During what was left of the late afternoon, and after having spent hours in the safari truck, Ceil began to relax. Already, sundowners were being arranged on a long, white-clothed trestle-table and, nearby, the camp-fire was well on its way to creating drama, not to mention safety.

During sundowner time, conversation, quite naturally, revolved around the game they had seen on the way to the Amboseli and the game they had seen in the park, not to mention the game they hoped, and expected, to see in the five days they were to spend here.

Snacks, with drinks, consisted of cubes of fried wilde-beest liver and smoked oysters on shortcrust biscuits. Feeling very much in Africa now, Ceil looked at the four Masai warriors who were there to guard the camp. How these human beings, with their spears, were expected to guard them from prowling wild animals, she shuddered to think. For the most part the warriors were very still and seemed almost to be staring into space, but now and then, just as though some signal had been noticed, they

broke into a chant. Unable to resist the fascination of
Ceil's silver-blonde hair, first one and then another man
came over to where she was sitting and began to touch
it.

Dinner was served in a leisurely but highly efficient
manner, and consisted of buffalo-tail soup, venison
steaks, fried onions, crisp baked potatoes and, for those
who wanted it, warm buttered bread. The wine was excellent, and all this was followed by a sponge pudding.

There was a smell of woodsmoke—that unmistakable
smell of Africa—and the animal noises were quite unbelievable, from the distant cough of a lion somewhere
to the barks of zebra and baboons. Until these re-
minders of the animals around them, it had not oc-
curred to Ceil that their camp might just not be welcome
around here, and she shivered.

By bedtime, Ceil was tired, but it was the kind of
bodily fatigue which was wonderful. Directly she and
Jonathan were inside their tent she said, 'Let me tell you
something, Jonathan. I could never have done this—
share a tent with you—had I not for some time been
sharing a house with you.'

'Since you didn't know what to expect, and didn't ask
what to expect, and imagining for a moment that you'd
not been sharing a house with me, you might well have
had no choice—and then what?' His tone was mocking.
'As it is, it's all turned out very well, don't you think?'

'I'm more concerned about the present moment than
what might have been,' she said fervently.

His blue gaze locked with hers. 'We know just enough
about each other to make it interesting. I enjoyed
watching you tonight, by the way. You were so thrilled

with everything—except perhaps when the Masai were excited by your hair. You handled it very well, though.'

'It's not every day I have strange men running their fingers through my hair! I found myself wishing I could understand what they were saying. I've made a promise to myself that I'm going to try to learn Swahili when I get back. I was surprised how well you were able to join in with the Masai people tonight. I heard them excitedly talking about what sounded to me to be—*fisi*,' she went on. 'What is *fisi*?'

'*Fisi* means hyena,' Jonathan told her. He went over to the table, poured himself some soda water, then, lifting the glass to his lips, he glanced at her over the rim. 'They have a word for lover—which is *mpenzi*.'

After a moment she said, 'Now, why did you have to say that? But let me say one thing; a situation in which I need to know the word for lover is not likely to arise—certainly not in this tent!'

'But the idea *is* seductive?' His eyes mocked her.

Trying to ignore the stab of excitement she felt, Ceil went over to where she had dropped her travel-bag and zipped it open. 'Jonathan, will you shower first?' she said. 'I'm exhausted and longing to climb into bed.'

'In that case, you shower first.' He almost dropped down on to his bed, then lay back with his hands behind his head and looked at her through his dark lashes.

Ceil was fully aware of the sexual tension between them. Even as she showered now her thudding heart wouldn't calm down. She found herself wondering what her mother would think of her right now—asking for trouble like this.

When she went back into the tent, she saw that Jonathan had fallen asleep. His face was innocently boyish and his breathing was slow and even. Her moody eyes went to his chin, which was firm and suggested that stubborn streak in him which she knew so well now.

She went to sit on her bed, wondering if he would wake up just at the very moment when she was getting into her pyjamas. Looking at him in the lamplight, she knew she was on thin, thin ice here. Without him in her life, she knew she would be lost, but she had no intention of getting involved in a casual affair, by which time his so-called worry and concern for her might well have petered out. Look at his affair with Xenia, she reasoned. Xenia was just a good friend, *now*.

Suddenly that boyish trace of a dimple appeared and, without opening his eyes, he said, 'Well? Don't you trust me?'

After a moment she answered, 'No.'

'Why?' He opened his eyes and turned his head so that he could look at her.

'Work it out for yourself.' Ceil shrugged her shoulders. 'I don't trust any man when it comes to sharing a tent.'

'I'm not any man—you should know that by now.'

'I'm not into having an affair,' she persisted.

'I don't want an affair. I'm in love with you and I want to marry you.' Jonathan stretched himself and she could see his body straining against his shirt.

'Oh, no! You're not going to do this to me, Jonathan Caister. How come, now that we're in this tent together, you want to marry me? Why haven't you asked me before?'

'Because your house keeps getting in the way.'

'What is it you don't like about that house? I think it's a gorgeous house.'

He pressed his palms on either side of his body and pushed himself up and off the high iron bed. 'Apart from the fact that it's as gorgeous as you are, since it's been continually worked on since the day you moved into it, as far as I'm concerned it's a house with no beginning and certainly no end—unless, of course, you want to go on living in it alone. Do you?'

'Maybe I want to be an artist,' she snapped. 'In any case, it did have a beginning. My great-aunt lived—and lived well—in it, and then she saw fit to leave it to me.'

'All that has nothing to do with me.' Jonathan shrugged off his shirt. 'I don't intend becoming an artist or working from home on a computer, simply because you inherited the house.'

Ceil was furious now. 'Back to the computer. Back to the house. Why can't we ever seem to get off these two subjects?'

She found herself talking to his back, as he made for the shower stall. By the time he returned she was in bed with her back turned to him. As he put out the lamp, the tent was plunged into darkness, and she immediately began to grope for the flashlight which he had insisted she keep near her. The touch of it reassured her, although she did not turn it on.

Almost as though the plunging of their tent into darkness was a signal, a hyena—or *fisi*—began to giggle crazily, and Ceil's hair stood on end.

'Are you nervous?' Jonathan's amused voice came to her in the darkness.

'I'm not so nervous, Jonathan, that I need a bed-mate,' she answered. 'I was just about asleep, actually.' She heard him laugh softly. 'Were you?'

CHAPTER THIRTEEN

'GOOD morning!'

It was a shout to awaken the dead, Ceil thought, turning over in her bed.

The next moment, the shout was followed by coffee being brought into the tent and placed on the table between the beds. Jonathan's bed was empty, and it was obvious that he had unzipped the tent and had gone to shower. All about the camp, canvas washstands and shower buckets were being filled with hot water. Glancing at her watch, Ceil saw that it was ten to five. Still half asleep, she closed her eyes and lay back. The coffee smelled divine, she thought contentedly.

'How did you sleep?'

At the sound of Jonathan's voice she turned her head and opened her eyes. A towel was draped around his hips and he was drying his dark hair with a small towel. In the morning half-light, she tried not to look at his strong legs.

'Fine. I woke up once or twice—and I'm sure I heard a lion—and close too.' She sat up and pushed her tangled silver-blonde hair back from her face.

'Anyway, good morning.' He came over to her and bent to touch his lips to her forehead.

'Oh, no, Jonathan. We don't kiss good morning at Mnarani, so why should we do so here?'

159

'Because you have the most amazing green eyes, and right now you look like a silky cat.'

The moment he said the word cat, Ceil realised that he regretted it. After coffee, he left the tent while she washed and dressed hurriedly. By the time she joined him she was wearing khaki trousers, a dark green top and a khaki jacket—all colours which emphasised her hair.

Game viewing proved to be wonderfully exciting, and after it was over and they were back at camp the Americans opted for a champagne breakfast, and for a moment Ceil thought they must be joking.

'Come on, Ceil, be a devil,' Evan laughed, and his eyes contained the kind of mockery which signified, If my clients want a champagne breakfast on safari, that's what they get.

After breakfast they lounged about the camp, sitting on canvas chairs facing Mount Kilimanjaro, which they could not see for mist.

'One day, I'll take you on another safari,' Jonathan was saying. 'When it comes to a safari, I prefer a more rough-and-ready approach.'

'What are you trying to prove?' Ceil found she wanted to mock him. 'How tough you are?'

'I don't have to prove anything—except, it would appear, that I love you.' His voice was curt.

'If you do, you're not going to prove it by luring me into having an affair at Amboseli. Just put that on record, will you?'

'I'm not asking you to have an affair with me,' he said.

'What are you asking me, then?' Her eyes were like cool green grapes.

'I'm asking you to sell your house and marry me and live in my house.'

'I have no intention of selling my house.'

'But you'll have an affair with me?' His voice, she thought, was only half teasing.

'I will not have an affair with you, Jonathan, and I have no intention of selling my house.'

'My house! That's so typical of you! Don't you ever think of anything but that house?' His eyes swept over her angrily.

'No, I don't. Even if by some fluke we were to get married, I would still think of that house. I have every intention of keeping it.'

'I see. Well, if by some fluke, as you so charmingly put it, you were to end up as my wife, *I* have no intention of living in it,' Jonathan declared.

'You don't have to mention marriage to pave the way for an affair here, Jonathan. In other words, there will be no sexual electricity on this safari.'

'I love you and I've asked you to marry me. I'm not thinking of mere sexual electricity, Ceil. You don't seem to realise that.'

After a moment she said, 'Jonathan, I'm more than just a little in love with you. But I keep asking myself how serious you really are about me. I mean, you don't seem to like *anything* about me—my ways, my work, my house. Have you come up with marriage as a means of getting me into bed with you while we're sharing a luxury tent together? Afterwards, would it be another case of "whatever we had going, Ceil and I, is over".

Another thing, you know how I feel about that house. You actually hate that house——'

'I don't hate the house! If you decide to marry me, however, I don't have to live in it, just because your romantic maiden aunt happened to have lived in it and left it to you to carry on where she left off! I'm quite capable of providing my wife with a home of our own choice.'

'And I'm supposed to fall in with your choice, in other words? I'm supposed to break down and drool over your house in Karen?'

'You distinctly told me you liked the house in Karen— or don't you remember?'

'I do remember. Supposing, though, we did get married, what am I supposed to do with *my* house? Pick it up and post it to England? I want to keep this house in the family.' She took a breath. 'I keep telling you, Jonathan, I love that house.'

Suddenly he got up and looked down at her. 'Well, if that's all you're capable of loving, I won't bother you.'

After he had left her, Ceil sat back and closed her eyes. Snatches of conversation, from the rest of the party, who were sitting nearby, kept invading her unsettled thoughts.

'Yes,' Evan was saying, 'it's a sad fact, but unfortunately ivory has been in great demand for thousands of years.'

Trying to blot out Evan's voice, Ceil thought, Jonathan's always hated that house. In the background Evan had begun to answer questions. 'I'm afraid the number of lodges and tented camps is increasing. There seems to be no thought for overcrowding.' Breaking off, he called out, 'Hey, Ceil, you look lonely sitting there in the mist all on your own. Where's Jonathan?'

She tensed immediately but, laughing lightly, she got to her feet. 'That's what I was just about to find out, Evan.'

Jonathan was stretched out on his bed and looked perfectly relaxed, which infuriated her, and she felt an irresistible urge to quarrel with him. 'I don't see why I should sit out there in the mist on my own, Jonathan. What's the matter with you?'

'You could have put your raincoat on or moved your chair and joined in the fun,' he pointed out. 'There's enough laughter going on outside. Why don't you go and join in?'

'In other words, I'm not wanted in here?'

'I keep telling you what I want.'

'I was just thinking out——'

'There in the mist on your own,' he cut in.

'Do you always have to be so insulting, Jonathan?' Her voice rose.

'Look, Ceil, this concerns something which is going on emotionally between two people—you and me. That's the important issue, not the house. You act like an indulged child with that house!'

'I don't! Why do you have to spoil this safari, Jonathan?' she demanded.

He swung his legs over the side of the bed and stood up. 'It's not my wish to spoil this safari.' He came over to her and took her by the shoulders. 'I've asked you to marry me. Can't we take it from there? Forget about the obstacles and see what happens.'

She did not resist when he put his arms right around her and drew her so close that his thighs were pressed against hers. At first he kissed her lingeringly and she felt she would be able to stop him from going further, but the reverse was happening. Feelings which she had not known existed within her were surging through her entire body. Realising that she would soon be unable to control the situation, she pulled away from him.

His blue eyes were impatient. 'Ceil, what's the matter with *you*?'

'I had a feeling similar to what you get when you're in a plane—you know, when the safety-belt signs start flashing. Don't do this to me, Jonathan. I'm not ready for it. I'm terribly confused right now.'

'I see. The safety-belt signs started flashing, and, very dutifully, you buckled your belt—just as you very dutifully intend to carry out your aunt's wish that you should go on living in her house for the rest of your life.'

'You seem to have very definite ideas on the kind of woman you want. She must be a doormat!' she flamed.

Why was she doing everything in her power to lose him? she asked herself.

Evan had come to the entrance of their tent, and called out, 'Everybody seems intent on going out again this morning. How do you two feel about viewing a large herd of elephants?'

Jonathan took a calming breath. 'I guess that will be fine, Evan. We'll be with you in a moment or two.' Looking at Ceil, he said, 'And I guess we're back where we started, right?'

*   *   *

The following day they were up early and drove out at sunrise and again at dusk—and so the safari continued. Ceil had little time to think of the computer, Frank or Yarda Lazar. What was more, she was enjoying herself, and so, by the looks of things, was Jonathan.

It was difficult to believe that Mount Kilimanjaro was only four hours from Nairobi and that canvas tents were the only barriers between those who occupied them and that wilderness beyond. Even though Evan had remarked that the number of lodges and tented camps was increasing, Africa was far from being tamed and was not about to be tamed either.

Although Jonathan made no attempt to make love to her, Ceil felt that he was very carefully leading her to a point where she would give in.

Sometimes, after lunch, he would fall asleep as they both rested in the tent. From her own bed, her moody green eyes would assess his masculinity. Tall, tanned and with intensely blue eyes, dark hair, regular features and a sensuous mouth, he thrilled and excited her as no man ever had. During his waking hours he was sexy and exciting to be with. In sleep, his face held a hint of boyish vulnerability.

While she liked a man to have strong and definite views on everything and found herself respecting his moods, she was not, she thought, about to permit him to rule her life.

On the last night there was a rather wild session, with the Americans pushing the pace. Drinks seemed to flow from a secret pub hidden amongst the acacia trees, and once, as Ceil was about to accept another from Evan, Jonathan said, 'Watch it, Ceil. Just don't overdo it!'

'I feel like another one,' she retorted.

A few moments later he stood up, reached for her hand and pulled her up beside him.

'How about some sleep?' He spoke lightly, but his eyes carried a warning.

They were shown by flashlight to their tent while, behind them, the laughter and talk continued around the orange flames of the campfire.

'Jonathan, just who do you think you are?' Ceil asked angrily. 'What makes you think you can decide when I should go to sleep? Another thing, why did you have to go and say that to me?'

He slipped his thumbs into the waistband of his khaki trousers and gave her a long look. 'What did I say?'

'You told me not to overdo the drinks. There was no excuse for that. I'm a sipper—damn it, I was hardly drinking!'

'Oh, cool it!' He took an impatient breath. 'I was looking after you.'

'I don't need looking after.'

'OK, you don't need looking after? Go back to the fire and get on your ear.'

'What infuriates me,' she went on, 'is that sometimes you carry on as if I've been especially created for you!'

The moment she'd uttered the words, she felt a sense of great loneliness. What was it she wanted? she asked herself. Why was she trying her level best to cut herself off from the only man she had ever loved?

'Oh, stop sniping!' Jonathan was really angry now. 'Do you ever stop to ask yourself what you're talking about? Despite your women's liberation approach to life, you *want* to be taken care of, let's face it. What's more, you want to be loved—to be made love to—*by me*. So did your aunt want to be loved and to be made love to—so you've implied, anyway. And yet what did she do? She went about it the hard way, right? She lived alone. She died alone. Why? Who was this man? I'm beginning to ask myself whose fault it was. His—or hers? I'm beginning to ask myself if she was anything like you, and I'm beginning to think she was.' He began to unbutton his shirt.

Outside, one of the Masai was shouting something, and by the sounds of it, a herd of elephants had decided to visit the camp.

Ceil's nerves sprang to life and her eyes flew to Jonathan's. The look he gave her was one of frank amusement.

'Why don't you go and have a look?' he asked. 'Are you afraid?'

'Fear has never been a problem in my life.' She stood hugging herself, cupping her elbows in her shaking hands.

For several moments they studied each other in the lamplight, then Jonathan came over to her just at the moment when she felt a cold slice of terror as a branch of an acacia tree snapped near to the tent.

'Come here, you little idiot.' His voice was soft and caressing, as he began to take off his shirt.

When he drew her close, moulding her body against his own, she did not resist him, even though she was fully aware of his excitement. His lips sought hers and almost immediately response flooded through her. She was conscious of his strength and felt suddenly young and very vulnerable as she found herself seeking that strength. Another part of her was excitedly analysing how it would be to belong to this man and to be made love to by him, whenever they both felt like it. She realised she was ready for this, and at the same time she was aware that she never did anything in life that was not of her own choosing.

She allowed the demands of her body to take over and her hands went to his warm back, after she had slipped them beneath the shirt he was wearing. For long, tense moments they stood this way, swaying slightly and almost drowning in their needs. Jonathan's hands slid down to her hips, crushing them so that they could fit closer against his own. A moment later he started to undress her, and while he did so her green eyes were slanted and dreaming.

'For all your big talk, Ceil,' he said softly, 'you're as fragile as a breeze laden with the scent of wild flowers, do you know that? I want to make love to you.'

'I want you to,' she said against his mouth.

He drew back. 'You're not going to feel terrible—afterwards?'

She shook her head, then felt a shock of pleasure as he picked her up and carried her over to her bed, where she watched him as he shed the rest of his clothing and then, as he reached for her again, she clung to him.

There was a rumble of thunder, followed by a flash of lightning and the spatter of raindrops as the storm which had been threatening for most of the day, broke over the tiny camp.

CHAPTER FOURTEEN

FRESHLY painted, pink-walled and white-pillared, her house awaited her—the tower to one side of it and linked by the newly built gallery. That tower, thought Ceil, was at the back of everything leading up to this point in her life. Mnarani was, in some ways, very much like the house which Jonathan had bought in Karen, the suburb of garden estates, and which was being restored to its original beauty.

So, she asked herself on their return from the Amboseli national park, what was the big fuss about? What did it matter which house they kept after they got married— but again, why couldn't it be *her* house?

There was no Frank to welcome them, and Saba went to some length to explain that he had looked for the cat every day, but with no success.

Before leaving the Amboseli, Ceil had made it clear that she had no intention of sharing her bed with Jonathan when they got back.

'I have to think,' she had explained.

'Think about what, Ceil? Whether I'm going to be permitted to make love to you again, or whether you're ready to become my wife?' His voice had been harsh with anger.

A week after they got back he knocked on her door one morning. 'Ceil? Are you awake?'

'Yes—I'm in bed, though. What is it, Jonathan?'

169

'May I come in?' he asked, with some impatience.

'I suppose so.'

As he came into the room he said, 'I've seen you in bed before—*and* with nothing on, in case you've forgotten. Have you?'

'I haven't forgotten.' Her voice was abrupt.

'Guess who's just walked in on long velvet legs and with the equivalent of a cat's black eye?' he asked, grinning.

'Oh, no-oo...!' she squealed. 'Where is he? I can't believe it, Jonathan!'

'Wait, I'll get him for you—that is, if he doesn't claw me to pieces.'

He returned carrying a purring and puffy-eyed Frank, and Ceil held out her arms. 'Oh, give him to me, Jonathan. Frank, you devil, where have you been? Just look at him!' She glanced up at Jonathan. 'I'll have to bath him. Can one bath a cat?'

Jonathan laughed. 'I haven't the faintest idea. I'll buy you a cat's comb in Nairobi today—there's a pet shop just round the corner from the office. Perhaps you could dip the comb in warm water and keep combing him. I'm sure he'll enjoy that, won't you, you Casanova?' He sat down on the side of Ceil's bed and began to stroke the cat, who obviously was growing tired of all this attention. He struggled to get off the bed and Ceil let him go.

'He must be starving,' she said. 'I'll get up and feed him.'

'I've already done that,' Jonathan told her.

Suddenly their eyes met. He was dressed for work and he smelled divine, she found herself thinking. It was just an understated cologne for men, but one which was obviously created to stir a woman's senses.

'How long are we going to go on like this?' he asked.

'I've had a lot on my mind, Jonathan. Until I get things sorted out I don't want us just to live together.'

He swore under his breath. '*I* don't want us just to live together—I want you to be my wife! Doesn't that mean anything to you?'

'It does, yes, but you're asking too much of me.'

He was seized by fury now and his eyes appeared a darker blue. 'What's asking too much of you? Selling this house and moving into my house in Karen?'

'In other words, Jonathan, if I marry you, I'll have to give up everything? I want to marry you.' She took an unsettled breath. 'I do—really! I don't mind living in your house in Karen. After all, it's going to be lovely when it's finished, and this furniture will fit in very well. It's...' She broke off and lifted her shoulders.

'Go on. It's—what?' Jonathan stood up and looked down at her.

'What it amounts to—is I want to marry you very much, and what's more, I'm willing to stay in—*live*— I'm willing to live in your house and come here for weekends. Saba will stay on as caretaker. We could even spend our holidays here. After all, there's a gorgeous pool and we could——'

'I want to spend my holidays travelling about, Ceil, not parked out here next to the pool and an adjacent game park!'

For a moment Ceil felt stark despair. Was it going to end, like this, over a house—well, *two* houses, actually!

Jonathan sat down again and she turned her shoulder on him.

'This is never going to work out.' Ceil felt like howling.

She heard him groan with exasperation, then he reached out for her and turned her round to face him.

'You're not going to bully me this way!' she flamed. 'Get away from me, Jonathan!'

'Look, keep the house, if it means so much to you. You'll always find suitable tenants—rent it out——'

'I'm not renting it out. Can you imagine the damage? People don't care when they rent houses.'

'Look,' Jonathan glanced at his watch, 'I've got to get going. I can't sit here all day. I'll be here until the end of the month, Ceil. Let me know what you intend doing.'

At the door he turned. 'I don't mind coming out here for the odd weekend, but that's as far as it goes.'

'You're very selfish, Jonathan!' she flung after him.

'Not half as selfish as you are!' he flung back.

They barely spoke for the next three days. In any case, Jonathan was busy working on plans which he brought home with him. Tension began to show in Ceil's face, and the memory of making love was always there to tantalise her.

The month was drawing to an end, and one evening after dinner Jonathan said on almost a note of indifference, 'Have you made up your mind about what you intend doing about this house?' He sat back and looked at her across the lamplit table. 'Permit me to say one thing, though. If you keep Mnarani to use for odd weekends—you know, a weekend here, a weekend there—it would soon become a white elephant. I should imagine, anyway, that once we're married and you have your own home, you'd soon tire of coming out here.'

'This *is* my home,' she argued stubbornly. 'Even if I don't live in it.'

He went on regardless, 'If it's the pool that's worrying you, I'm having a pool put in. In fact, I've already spoken to the guy...'

'How stupid can you be?' she flamed. 'It's not just the pool! You're so hard, Jonathan.'

'Maybe you're just being hard on yourself.'

'This house has so many memories,' she persisted. 'I could never sell it.'

'What do these memories hold for you?' he exploded. 'Nothing! Except, perhaps, memories of the day you found out you'd inherited it...the day you moved in. You barely knew your great-aunt—you told me that yourself. She was a——'

'She was a *legend*,' Ceil finished for him. 'She wanted me to have the house.'

'Is that your answer, then? You want to live out a legend?' His voice was hard and demanded an answer.

She felt absolutely stifled. What right had he to do this to her?

'My answer is this,' she told him. 'Once we're married, we make the house in Karen our permanent home. I intend keeping this house. You don't have to spend weekends here, let alone holidays. I'll come out here on my own from time to time.'

'I won't have you coming out here to stay on your own.'

'And yet,' her voice was bitter, 'you distinctly told me you'd be here to the end of the month, which means you're on the brink of walking out of this house and leaving me alone. I can't understand you! You're a mystery. Apart from anything else, this house is an investment, Jonathan, and I'll keep it until I'm ready to sell it. That's my answer. Saba will act as caretaker and I'll visit it—whenever I wish.'

She watched him as he stood up and came round to her chair. Reaching for her hand, he pulled her up beside him.

'Sometimes I ask myself whose side this house is on,' he said softly. He tilted her face towards his own. 'Keep your house, Ceil, but—for God's sake—and I mean that—let's stop fighting about it.'

As he gathered her into his arms, she felt a rush of excitement and clung to him.

'I've wanted you so much, since we got back from Amboseli,' he said.

As he kissed her she said against his mouth, 'I hate it when we fight.'

A moment later they broke apart as the lights of a car lit up the pool area, then swept into view and pulled up in front of the steps leading to the veranda. Ceil's breath caught in her throat as she recognised Yarda Lazar's car. He got out and slammed the door, and as he came up the steps he said, 'So you're back? Saba said you'd gone to the Amboseli. You didn't mention it last time we had lunch together. I thought I'd just drive out and see for myself what's going on in the world.' Glancing at Jonathan, he went on, 'We met at the croc park.'

'I have a bad memory.' Jonathan's voice was like ice, and then, without looking at Ceil, he went towards the open french doors which led into the lounge.

After he had gone Ceil said angrily, 'How dare you turn up here—and at this time of day? What do you want?'

Yarda Lazar shrugged. 'All I'm asking is for you to let me talk to you. Actually, I'm going away soon. I know a place where you can enjoy some cheese and a glass of wine. I've also got some items of news about Abdel Khaled that's going to make your hair stand on end, and by the end of our little chat if I haven't convinced you to stop working for him I'll be more than just a little surprised.'

'No! Just leave.'

'I think your fiancé should know what you're into. Get him to come out here and we'll all talk.'

The last thing Ceil wanted was for Jonathan, with his quick temper, and Yarda Lazar to get together.

'I'll get a jacket,' she said. 'Then after you've had your say, leave me alone. I've had enough of all this.'

Jonathan was in his study and standing at the door. Ceil said, 'Jonathan, I'm going with Yarda. I must.'

He did not look up. 'You do as you feel best. You always do, anyway.' He appeared callously indifferent.

Yarda took her to a place called Flashier Version, where people were dancing to loud and funky music. In fact, everything seemed drowned by the electronic music and Ceil wondered how they were going to talk. He ordered cheese and wine, but she did not touch hers, and he did not seem to notice as he repeated a lot of what he had already told her.

'Let's dance,' he said, after a while.

'I didn't come here to dance,' she told him.

He stood up and came round and reached for her. 'One dance, then we'll go. You know the story now. I'm going to blow the lid off Computa-mate. You won't see me again.'

Reluctantly, Ceil stood up. 'One dance, then take me home. I mean that!'

She danced away from him and, to keep him pleasant, put on a show of enjoying herself.

Jonathan, she discovered when she got home, was out, and she felt a spurt of anger mingled with disappointment in him. She might have needed him, she found herself thinking. She might have had to phone him from Flashier Version to ask him to come and rescue her from Yarda—and yet here he was, out!

He arrived soon afterwards, and looking at him with accusing green eyes, she said, 'I didn't know you were out.'

'Did you expect me to stay in?' He seemed to be struggling with his anger.

As it was Saturday, he did not go to work the following morning. After a restless night Ceil woke early, and as she lay brooding about Yarda Lazar she realised that she would have to tell Jonathan everything.

Some time later she heard him dive into the pool, which was now a glittering blue shape in the garden and in constant use, since they both enjoyed swimming. Fifteen minutes later, wearing her *kanga* over a black swimsuit, she went out to the pool.

'You're up nice and early!' she called, as though nothing had happened the night before.

'Well, I wasn't out dancing at the Flashier Version last night, after all.' Jonathan hoisted himself out of the water and reached for a towel.

Ceil was holding a glass of orange juice which she had brought out with her, and as she lifted the glass to her lips she looked at him over the rim. A moment later she said, 'You must have followed us, in that case?'

'For sure I followed you.' His eyes met and held hers. 'The girl I'm in love with—and what's more, the girl I'm going to marry—going off with some creep!'

'Why didn't you just stop me—going off with him?' she blazed. 'It would have been more honest.'

'Talking about being more honest, you want to examine yourself!' he retorted.

Ceil let that slide and tried to ignore the feeling of empty despair inside her, as she sat down on a straw basket chair and crossed her long, slim legs. She took another sip of her orange juice and felt like choking.

'I've come to the conclusion that it will be better to leave you to get on with your life in your pink fortress,' Jonathan continued. 'I've got better things to do.'

Ceil felt she should explain. 'In a way, Jonathan, Yarda Lazar's trying to blackmail me into meeting him so that he can get at me for coming up with the wrong Computa-mate,' she told him. 'Yarda's marriage ended on the rocks. He says he's found out that there's another side to Computa-mate. A kind of call-girl set-up, I suppose you could call it—and, even worse, a number of girls have disappeared. He says he's been doing a lot of investigation and is about to blow the lid off Computa-mate. How he tracked me down, I don't know. As you're aware, only my telephone number, along with my second name, Grace, and my Nairobi post-box appears on the letterhead.' She took a deep breath. 'He says that a lot of stupid and innocent girls have ended up being—often unwillingly—the playmates of wealthy men, and, as I say, some of them have disappeared without trace. I'm terribly distressed.' She was on the point of tears, but she did not want him to know.

'Why did you keep this to yourself?' His impatient blue eyes swept over her.

'For the simple reason that you had something against this work from the beginning. Call it pride, if you like, for want of a better word.'

'Did he phone to ask for an appointment—and, like an idiot, you agreed?'

'No.'

'What, then?'

'I'm not here to be cross-examined, Jonathan—but in any case, he just walked in—like you always said someone would walk in one day. I'd been out in the garden and I forgot to close and lock the wooden door afterwards. There, does that satisfy you? For obvious reasons I thought it best not to tell you. After all, you've been preaching enough about it.'

'I wish I could understand you! I wish I knew what makes you tick, Ceil!' Jonathan spoke in a carefully modulated voice, but this was worse than if he had shouted at her.

'I was going to tell you everything today.'

'Today? Why didn't you tell me all this last night?' he demanded.

'There'd have been trouble if I'd told you last night!' she flamed. 'I didn't want a scene. Let's face it, there would have been a scene—ending in who knows what? One of you getting hurt.'

'The point is, you should have told me from the very beginning,' said Jonathan angrily.

'I knew what you'd have to say...I *told* you so!'

'Don't use that tone with me, Ceil. Did it ever occur to you that I care very much about what happens to you? That I'd want to help you? Why do you think I suggested sharing a house with you in the first place?'

In an attempt to try and deal with her humiliation she said, 'Ever since I met you, you've tried to manipulate me.' Tension showed in her face. 'If anybody has conquered the art of using domination, anger and even charm to get his own way, that person is you, Jonathan. I don't tell you how to run your life! Do I now?'

He came towards her chair and pulled her up in no uncertain manner.

'You'll spill my orange juice,' she said, hurting inside.

'It's no problem. Get rid of it.' He took the glass from her and dropped it on the lawn, then took her into his arms. 'Now, let's stop hurting each other, before it's too late.'

Still hurting and humiliated, she said, 'I suppose what *should* have happened is that I should have run straight to you... Jonathan, you were right about Abdel Khaled and his computer services. You were right about keeping the security gates fastened. I'm sorry, Jonathan, for being such a little fool. I should have known better...'

Suddenly he released her. 'I don't have to put up with this,' he growled, and strode away.

After he had made his way to the house, to spite him Ceil swam twelve lengths in the glittering pool, then she lay in the sun and looked at the sky, with tear-sheened green eyes.

What's got into me since I came to Kenya? she asked herself. What is it about this house? Have I, finally, lost Jonathan?

Like your great-aunt Ceil, this is what you wanted. Right? Now you can get on with your life in your pink fortress.

'I don't want to be like her,' she whispered. In some ways she wished she had never been left the house, and yet it was a lovely old house with a great deal of charm. What was more, it had brought Jonathan and herself together. To keep Jonathan, though, she would have to let Mnarani go—if it was not too late.

CHAPTER FIFTEEN

CEIL phoned Abdel Khaled the following day and told him that she could no longer work for him, and requested that he make arrangements to have the computer and office equipment removed from her house.

'It must be today, Mr Khaled.' Her voice was firm.

Without asking her what her reasons were for this move he answered curtly, 'Today is impossible.'

'Make it possible. Everything must go today! I no longer wish to run Computa-mate. It's complicating my life and, it would appear, the lives of others. No doubt you know what I'm talking about.'

'At great inconvenience to myself, and others, I will arrange for everything to be collected today—and by everything, Miss Downing, I mean all paperwork included—no matter whether anything is pending or not. I want everything to come back to me.'

Later in the morning she received a phone call from Yarda Lazar.

'Things are beginning to look up,' he told her. 'Khaled knows I've got him pinned to the wall. Look, I feel like celebrating my victory. How about lunch?'

'It's impossible. I'm going away—in a few minutes, actually.' She decided to lie. 'Besides, I no longer work for Computa-mate, so having lunch seems pointless.' Directly she had put the phone down she went out to the garden, where she fought for some serenity in her life.

The following morning she put Mnarani on the market and then made arrangements to go to Diani Beach—simply because Jonathan had spoken about its beauty in Mombasa. Then she phoned her mother in England and explained the position to her.

'But I thought you loved the house, Ceil?' her mother exclaimed. 'The photos you've sent are beautiful. We were very impressed.' She laughed lightly. 'Jealous, actually.'

'Well, yes, I do,' said Ceil, 'but Jonathan's house is just as nice. The work on it is practically complete. I also wanted to let you know that I'll be going away for a few days. I've been so busy lately that I look a wreck, and I don't want to look like that on my wedding-day.'

She had agreed to marry Jonathan, but had made it clear that she was going to keep the house—probably with a view to letting it to suitable tenants. After much thought, however, she had reached the conclusion that it would be better to part with Mnarani and finish with it.

After she had given her mother the name and telephone number of the hotel at Diani Beach she phoned Tom Mzima to ask him to pick her up and take her to the airport, and then to meet her again when she got back.

Just when she was giving up hope of having someone call for the computer, desk and filing cabinet, a small van arrived from Nairobi.

Before leaving for the airport with Tom, she wrote a letter to Jonathan.

I have to get away. I hope you understand. With elaborate apologies for walking out on you like this. *Please* understand, Jonathan. I'll be back on Tuesday. I love you very much. Ceil.

Diani Beach was everything she needed in her life right now. At night there was nothing but blackness, broken only by the beach strip, which was softly luminous. Coconuts, bananas and citrus were being developed on the land immediately behind the beach, and elsewhere there were stretches of original forest.

There was time to think and time to sort out her emotions. Perhaps she had made a mistake by deciding to sell the house, after all, especially as Jonathan had agreed that she should keep it. The biggest mistake, though, had been in allowing Jonathan to make love to her in the camp at Amboseli, for since then they had both been even more strung-up, strained and touchy— both of them craving more lovemaking but neither wanting to slip into the category of living together.

She thought about the houses—hers and his. What difference did it make what house they lived in? Besides, she had to be strictly honest with herself. She did like his house in Karen. The garden was quite large—whereas the garden at Mnarani was huge and needed to be utilised as a smallholding farm, and neither she nor Jonathan would have time for that. Still, she was miserable, and, what was more, she was going to go on feeling miserable. She knew that.

On the third night, there was a knock on her door. She had just got out of her bath and was going to dress for dinner. Slipping into a robe, she called out, 'Yes? Who is it?'

'With elaborate apologies, Ms Downing, room service.'

The sarcastic answer came from Jonathan, and, for a moment, sheer despair raced through her. How on earth had he known where to find her?

Opening the door, she said, 'Jonathan, why did you follow me? All I wanted was a few measly days by myself!'

He came into her room, and she closed the door and stood looking at him, as he slipped his flight-bag from his shoulder and dropped it on to the floor.

'You know something? You're unbelievable! Walking out on me like that!' He went to the small bar refrigerator and poured himself a drink.

'Did it ever strike you that I might have wanted to think?' she asked.

'You wanted to think, huh?' He took a swallow of his drink. 'Let me give you some advice, Ceil, never do a thing like that again. I wouldn't do it to you. That's something else you can think about!'

'You must have got in touch with Tom,' she guessed. 'Did you?'

'No, I didn't need to get in touch with Tom.' He put his glass down and got out of his jacket, then began to undo the buttons of his shirt. 'Your mother phoned me.'

Ceil's eyes widened in shock. 'Why? Is something wrong?'

'Nothing's wrong. She told me you'd put Mnarani on the market. She was amazed I didn't know. *I* was amazed I didn't know, actually. Instead of feeling really good about this piece of news, I began to feel really bad. Why didn't we talk it over?' His blue eyes raked her face.

'Why? Why, Jonathan? You stand there and have the nerve to ask why! It's all you've ever wanted, let's face it, so what difference would it have made?'

'After you left I also had time to think, and I came up with the conclusion that I've been unreasonable about the house. There was no reason why we couldn't have kept it as a weekend house. After all, it meant a lot to you and you wanted to keep it in the family. I can see that now.'

'Well, it's too late now, isn't it?' Her voice carried a faint sneer. 'Too late, Jonathan. Anyway, what did my mother want? She knew I'd be away. I just can't understand her—and what's more I can't understand why you should come all this way if there's nothing wrong.'

'Your father wants to buy the house.'

'Buy the house? You must be joking!' Ceil felt almost faint.

'I'm not joking. I had to phone every estate agent in Nairobi, until I found out which one was handling the sale. Apparently your father and your uncle Peter want to buy the house and—along with their respective wives, of course—want to come out to Kenya to be near you and to raise chickens and grow nice things to eat. Naturally, the sun plays a big part in all this.'

Despite anything she could do about it, Ceil began to laugh. 'I don't believe it! They all want to settle out here together?'

'Yes. To use your mother's expression, they've been putting out feelers ever since you left England, but they didn't want to let you know, in case things went wrong.

They want you to keep the house until they're able to work things out. Your mother says the tower will be used as a guesthouse for your brother and his family when they visit.'

Ceil began to cry. 'I've been through so much over that house,' she sobbed. 'You'll never know what you did to me, Jonathan.'

'I'm sorry.' He came over to her and took her into his arms. 'It's just that I felt you were obsessed—it seemed to mean so much more to you than anything else in life. Besides, I wanted to be the one to provide a house. I've told your old lady——'

'My mother,' she corrected, beginning to laugh again.

'I've told your mother to get a move on and come out here, so that we can get on with that wedding.' He lifted her chin with the tips of his fingers. 'What do you say?'

'I agree. And so, like my great-aunt Ceil after whom I was named, I will adorn the long veranda and the lawns of Mnarani with tables—one of her many tables—and chairs, and we'll have the kind of garden-party reception she would totally approve of. I can see it all. Dusky-pink bougainvillaea——'

'Let me know when you're finished—I want to make love to you,' Jonathan said against her lips.

'I'm finished.' Ceil drew back and looked into his eyes. 'But in any case I've learned one thing—you have a knack of getting your own way!'

AUGUST 1991 HARDBACK TITLES

——— ROMANCE ———

No Gentle Seduction *Helen Bianchin*	3540	0 263 12874 1
Heart in Flames *Sally Cook*	3541	0 263 12875 X
Once a Cheat *Jane Donnelly*	3542	0 263 12876 8
Dreams are for Living *Natalie Fox*	3543	0 263 12877 6
With Strings Attached *Vanessa Grant*	3544	0 263 12878 4
Barrier to Love *Rosemary Hammond*	3545	0 263 12879 2
Second-Best Husband *Penny Jordan*	3546	0 263 12880 6
Dance for a Stranger *Susanne McCarthy*	3547	0 263 12881 4
Moon Over Mombasa *Wynne May*	3548	0 263 12882 2
The Final Touch *Betty Neels*	3549	0 263 12883 0
Far from Over *Valerie Parv*	3550	0 263 12884 9
Hijacked Honeymoon *Eleanor Rees*	3551	0 263 12885 7
The Dark Side of Desire *Michelle Reid*	3552	0 263 12886 5
Playing by the Rules *Kathryn Ross*	3553	0 263 12887 3
Twin Torment *Sally Wentworth*	3554	0 263 12888 1
Jungle Enchantment *Patricia Wilson*	3555	0 263 12889 X

MASQUERADE *Historical*

Perdita *Sylvia Andrew*	M269	0 263 12958 6
Set Free My Heart *Sarah Westleigh*	M270	0 263 12959 4

MEDICAL ROMANCE

A Special Challenge *Judith Ansell*	D187	0 263 12952 7
Heart in Crisis *Lynne Collins*	D188	0 263 12953 5

LARGE PRINT

Unlikely Cupid *Catherine George*	447	0 263 12691 9
Anything for You *Rosemary Hammond*	448	0 263 12692 7
Heart on Fire *Charlotte Lamb*	449	0 263 12693 5
Blind Passion *Anne Mather*	450	0 263 12694 3
Devil to Pay *Susan Napier*	451	0 263 12695 1
A Little Moonlight *Betty Neels*	452	0 263 12696 X
No Way to Begin *Michelle Reid*	453	0 263 12697 8
Without Knowing Why *Jessica Steele*	454	0 263 12698 6

SEPTEMBER 1991 HARDBACK TITLES

ROMANCE

The Ends of the Earth *Bethany Campbell*	3556	0 263 12906 3
Tempestuous Reunion *Lynne Graham*	3557	0 263 12907 1
When Love Returns *Vanessa Grant*	3558	0 263 12908 X
Winter Destiny *Grace Green*	3559	0 263 12909 8
African Assignment *Carol Gregor*	3560	0 263 12910 1
Dangerous Infatuation *Stephanie Howard*	3561	0 263 12911 X
A Cure for Love *Penny Jordan*	3562	0 263 12912 8
Lethal Attraction *Rebecca King*	3563	0 263 12913 6
Deep Water *Marjorie Lewty*	3564	0 263 12914 4
Istanbul Affair *Joanna Mansell*	3565	0 263 12915 2
Roarke's Kingdom *Sandra Marton*	3566	0 263 12916 0
Stormy Relationship *Margaret Mayo*	3567	0 263 12917 9
Undercover Affair *Lilian Peake*	3568	0 263 12918 7
Contract to Love *Kate Proctor*	3569	0 263 12919 5
Ghost of the Past *Sally Wentworth*	3570	0 263 12920 9
Hong Kong Honeymoon *Lee Wilkinson*	3571	0 263 12921 7

MASQUERADE *Historical*

Pink Parasol *Sheila Walsh*	M271	0 263 12960 8
The Arrogant Cavalier *Olga Daniels*	M272	0 263 12961 6

MEDICAL ROMANCE

Medical Decisions *Lisa Cooper*	D189	0 263 12954 3
Deadline Love *Judith Worthy*	D190	0 263 12955 1

LARGE PRINT

When the Devil Drives *Sara Craven*	455	0 263 12715 X
Breaking the Ice *Kay Gregory*	456	0 263 12716 8
Payment Due *Penny Jordan*	457	0 263 12717 6
Master of Marshlands *Miriam Macgregor*	458	0 263 12718 4
Land of Dragons *Joanna Mansell*	459	0 263 12719 2
Flight of Discovery *Jessica Steele*	460	0 263 12720 6
The Devil's Kiss *Sally Wentworth*	461	0 263 12721 4
Valley of the Devil *Yvonne Whittal*	462	0 263 12722 2